Murder & Mischief

A Victorian Crime Thriller

Carol Hedges

Little G Books

For Irene

About the Author

Carol Hedges is the successful British author of 20 books for teenagers and adults. Her writing has received much critical acclaim, and her novel Jigsaw was shortlisted for the Angus Book Award and longlisted for the Carnegie Medal.

Carol was born in Hertfordshire, and after university, where she gained a BA (Hons.) in English Literature & Archaeology, she trained as a children's librarian. She worked for the London Borough of Camden for many years subsequently re-training as a secondary school teacher when her daughter was born.

The Victorian Detectives series

Diamonds & Dust
Honour & Obey
Death & Dominion
Rack & Ruin
Wonders & Wickedness
Fear & Phantoms
Intrigue & Infamy
Fame & Fortune
Desire & Deceit

Acknowledgments

Many thanks to Gina Dickerson, of RoseWolf Design, for another superb cover, and to my editor and beta reader.

I also acknowledge my debt to all those amazing Victorian novelists for lighting the path through the fog with their genius. Unworthily, but optimistically, I follow in their footsteps.

Murder & Mischief

A Victorian Crime Thriller

It is January1868 and finally, it has stopped snowing. For days, big white flakes have fallen unceasingly out of a slate-grey sky, sculpting the city in sparkling whiteness, as if it was part of some monstrous wedding cake. Overnight the temperature has dropped, and there are now glossy crusts of ice on the snowy, white mounds.

Waking in their shared bedroom on the second floor of the Hampstead family home, Jacob and Edmund Barrowclough, sons of James William Malin Barrowclough, rush to the window to contemplate the pristine new world that stretches all the way to the horizon, just waiting to be explored. The light has a raw sharp edge. They exchange gleeful grins.

"Brekker first," says Jacob, senior scion of the Barrowclough dynasty. He heads for the ottoman, where clean clothes have been laid out, in readiness for the new day. Jacob pulls his nightshirt over his head and begins to dress himself. Three years at Eton, learning Latin, Greek and social superiority has gifted him with an independence still lacking in his younger brother, who has only just started at Eton and whose plump fingers still hesitate over tapes and buttons.

"Here, Eddie, let me do it," Jacob says, briskly buttoning the boy into his woollen combinations before hauling him into a shirt and thick herringbone tweed knickerbockers.

Once dressed, booted, and with their excitement mounting, the two boys clatter noisily downstairs to the crimson-papered dining room, where servants are laying the table ready for the family breakfast.

Jacob advances on the sideboard, where serried ranks of toast are lined up ready, and a dish of succulent fat sausages hisses over a small flame, awaiting consumption. He grabs a couple of slices of toast, and hands one to his brother. "Come on, let's go straight out," he says. "We can grab some sangers later. The kitchen skivvies won't mind keeping them hot for us ~ eh, Bartram?" he adds, addressing the chief footman, who smiles falsely and nods, because he knows it is not worth losing his place by checking the behaviour of the Barrowclough brothers. Especially the cocky older one.

With a jaunty air, Master Jakes (as he is known to the servants) heads for the conservatory door and wrenches it open. Then, accompanied by Master Edmund, he bursts out into the crisp silent whiteness of the snowy garden. Scooping up a handful of snow, he moulds it into a ball, which he throws at his brother.

"Race you to the spinney," he yells, and sets off at speed towards the small, darkly wooded copse at the far end of the grounds. It leads, via a gate, onto the vast wilderness of the Heath.

****

Hill House. A good name, thinks Detective Inspector Lachlan Greig of Scotland Yard, as he steps out of Heath Street Underground Station and begins to make his way, accompanied by one of the Hill House manservants, up the steep, snowy road towards the frozen Whitestone horse-pond. The winter sunlight is yellow and gluey. His breath comes out in foggy clouds. He is grateful for the warm woollen socks, knitted by his sister in Scotland and sent as a Christmas present.

Greig has left his wife and unborn child warm and safe in front of a roaring fire, and here he is, toiling up the snow-strewn road, past shops still full of seasonal fare and festive goods, and houses with Christmas candles in their windows. Just his bad luck, he thinks, to be on duty with a skeleton staff of men, post the Christmas celebrations. He was actually on the point of returning to hearth and home, as nothing much was happening in the world of serious crime, when the manservant from Hill House had arrived at the front desk with an urgent summons for a detective to come back with him at once, as 'something terrible' had occurred.

They reach the top of Heath Street, where Greig pauses to draw breath. Small children, some in ragged clothes, have emerged from the cottages to slide on the ice, or throw snowballs at passing trade carts. Some have wooden skates tied onto their boots and have launched out bravely onto the ice.

"This way sir, if you please," the manservant says, leading him towards an iron gate behind which stands a tall, white, flat-fronted mansion. They crunch across snowy gravel and mount the steps to the front door. The manservant opens the door and tells Greig to wait in the hallway. He then disappears into the house. Greig waits. Ahead of him he sees great vases of bright-berried holly, paper chains, ornate gold-framed mirrors on the dark papered walls and a rosewood side table full of cards. The air smells of oranges, cloves and money.

A few minutes later, the manservant returns. He opens the front door. "Mr. Barrowclough says you are to go straight round to the back. He will meet you there," he says, before shutting the door firmly in Greig's face.

Greig shrugs. The attitude of the rich and powerful towards the upholders of law and order used to grate, but no longer bothers him any more. He has learned that the servants of the monied class inherit the same snooty casualness from their employers. The manservant in this case has barely exchanged a half-dozen sentences with him since they began their journey from Scotland Yard. It is what it is though and, as he may need to question him later, there is no point in making tart observations to his employer on the behaviour of his staff.

Greig reminds himself that at the end of the day, he has a job to do, and do it he will, to the best of his ability.

So, pausing to scrape the muck and compacted snow from his boots onto the edge of the newly cleaned top step, he walks to the rear of the property, where he spies a well-built man in his mid-forties, clean shaven, with sharp features, and pale blue eyes that regard Greig with barely veiled hostility. He is clad in an expensive handmade wool overcoat, tweed cap and gaiters. Foregoing social pleasantries, he nods a brief greeting before striding out across the snowy expanse of lawn.

"You took your time getting here," he remarks. Greig notes the slight northern accent underneath the admonitory tone. "Now then, officer," the man continues, over his shoulder, "I hope you have a strong stomach. Prepare yourself for a shock."

Frowning, Greig follows him, his feet sinking into the soft snow. The lawn is criss-crossed with numerous footprints, but Barrowclough steers a straight path towards a spinney of young trees at the far end of the garden. He reaches it and opens a small wooden gate.

"There," he says, gesturing. "This is what I want you to see. Over by the fence."

Greig stares in the direction of the pointing finger. There is something white, just beyond the trees. A shape. Round body and round head against the grey sky and dark leafless branches. Top hat surmounting it. Puzzled, he turns to face Barrowclough. "A snowman? You brought me here to look at a snowman?"

The man laughs harshly. "Take a closer look, officer, why don't you," he says, his eyes narrowing. "I don't think you'll see many snowmen like this one."

Greig walks up to the white shape. He observes that it is not so much a made snowman, as something covered by snow that has taken on the likeness of one. It has a strange, flat face, a penny for an eye. He leans forward, intrigued. Next minute, he starts back, uttering an exclamation of horror. There is a gelid human eye

4

glaring back at him through the hole where the second penny ought to have been; a fragment of greyish cloth pokes through the snow covering the body.

"There it is, officer," Barrowclough says grimly. "This is what my two boys discovered when they ventured out to play in the snow this morning. They found the 'snowman' and decided to throw snowballs at it. As boys will. Then they went closer and saw it had pennies for eyes. They removed one of the pennies and that is what was underneath. Of course, they came and told me at once, but I didn't believe them ~ boys, you know. But they insisted, so at last I came to see for myself.

"It seems that someone, or maybe a gang, broke through the fence, trespassed into my grounds, and then encased a man in snow and left him to die in my spinney, propped against a tree. It has terrified my two sons out of their wits. They have had to be put straight to bed. I have not dared tell their mother as she is delicate. I got my manservant to make sure there wasn't anything else untoward left anywhere, but he found nothing. Then I sent for you."

Greig has his notebook open by now and is making rapid observations. He notes that the ground all around and beyond the snow figure has been well trodden down, making it unlikely that the footprints of the original trespasser(s) could be identified. Mentally, he curses Barrowclough for not realising that this was a crime scene and leaving it untouched for the professionals to deal with.

"And now, officer," the man continues, "I demand that this … this abomination be removed. I want it gone by the end of the day. If not before. I presume you have places where you store dead bodies? I do not want my boys to see it ever again. I do not want my wife to know of its existence. I don't want my servants coming out to gawp and spreading the tale round the neighbourhood. I don't know who this person is, nor why he has been put here. Do you understand me?"

Greig nods. "Indeed, I understand you perfectly, sir. I shall make arrangements for the body to be taken to the nearest police mortuary as soon as possible. I must warn you, though, that we may have to trouble you again once it has been thawed out ~ it is possible that the person might be known to you or a member of your household."

"I think that extremely unlikely."

"Nevertheless," Greig continues calmly, "there must be a reason why this place was chosen above all others, sir. We often find that there is a link to a crime and its location. It may be so in this case."

Barrowclough bridles. "I assure you, officer, I can think of nobody of my acquaintance who would do such a damned vile thing. I have no enemies ~ business rivals, I admit, but none who'd stoop to such a wicked act." He studies the silent white figure. "No, this is clearly the work of some madman. You would be better off inquiring at one of the local lunatic asylums. That is the most likely source of this outrage."

Greig closes his notebook. The day he takes advice from a member of the public (especially one of the arrogant, new-monied variety) is the day he hangs up his detecting boots. "I will bid you good day, sir," he says calmly. "My men will call round as soon as possible to collect the body and, as I indicated, either myself or one of my officers will be in touch with you in due course. If you would care to give me your card, I can make sure that the initial contact takes place at your office away from your family, if that is what you prefer."

Reluctantly, Barrowclough leads the way back to the conservatory. His whole demeanour is of offended outrage. He indicates that Greig should wait outside once more while he fetches a card. Having handed it over and reiterated once again that it is nothing to do with him, he makes a brief bow and closes the conservatory door, leaving Greig to make his solo way back to the street and thence down the hill towards the underground station and his chilly office at Scotland Yard.

But first, there is somewhere else he decides to visit. It is a bitterly cold day, and he has been standing around in the open air for some time. Winter stalks the streets. Barrowclough can wait. The 'snowman' is clearly going nowhere. A cup of tea and a piece of cake is called for. And a warmup in front of a roaring fire. And maybe, if he plays his cards right, some useful local gossip.

Greig heads swiftly past the station and turns left into Flask Walk, coming to a halt outside a small brightly lit restaurant. The swinging tea-pot sign proclaims that he has reached the Lily Lounge Tearoom, prop. L. Marks (Mrs). He pushes open the door and enters.

Lilith Marks (the 'Mrs' is an honorary soubriquet, as its owner has never married) is an imposing woman. She wears black ~ a social indication that she is a widow (she isn't). Her dark hair, now streaked with grey, is pinned in serpentine coils around her head. She is the owner of a chain of popular tea-rooms dotted around the capital, and a number of refreshment concessions in several big West End department stores. Her team of bakers and confectioners also cater for private functions, weddings and parties.

It all is a very far cry from her origins, when her 'customers' would have left their money on the nightstand before making their way furtively out into the night-time street. Few observing her today would ever guess at her origins. Greig knows them, mainly because Lilith was instrumental in the past in saving the life of his wife Josephine and rescuing her from the clutches of an evil Romanian Countess.

Today, as he hoped, Lilith is presiding personally behind the wooden counter, watching as her waitresses bustle to and fro, carrying trays laden with sandwiches and luscious cakes. Every table is full, and the air resonates with excited female chatter, for many shops have begun their January sales, and there is much to show and discuss.

Lilith's eyes light up as she spies the tall figure of Lachlan Greig enter. "Lachlan," she exclaims, hurrying out from behind the counter. "What a lovely surprise. But you are alone? Where is Josephine? Is she well? I hope nothing has befallen her."

"Everything is quite well," Greig reassures her with a smile. "And we have both enjoyed the Christmas cake you so kindly sent us. I am here, you might say, in an official capacity." He closes his mouth and gives her a significant look.

Lilith reads and interprets it. She beckons to one of the staff. "Cassie, can you take my place at the cash desk?" she requests. "I am just stepping down to the kitchen for a short break."

Greig follows Lilith down to the warm spice-scented kitchen. Lilith sets the kettle onto the stove, selects two mugs and reaches for the teapot and caddy. While she is thus engaged, Greig reads silently though his notes, circling various sentences. Once they are both settled on either side of the well-worn wooden table, a mug, and a piece of gingerbread on a plate in front of each of them, he tells her about his visit to Hill House. Lilith listens intently, her eyes fixed upon his face. When Greig has finished, she stirs her tea in a thoughtful manner for a few seconds.

"That is a frightful thing, Lachlan ~ I can well imagine those children must have been terrified out of their wits. I used to see the boys out and about with their old nurse, but recently, since they have both been away at boarding school, I haven't seen either of them. Nor the nurse. The family keeps themselves to themselves. Nobody from Hill House has set foot in my tea-rooms over the festive period.

"I have to say that there have been rumours about the state of the marriage ~ she comes from the upper classes, whereas I gather his family were in business somewhere in the Midlands. Mind, in a small place like this, people tend to gossip ~ yes, even I admit to the cardinal sin myself. Minding other folks' business keeps us interested in the world. Well, I will certainly keep my ears and eyes open. Such a thing is bound to become the topic of conversation once it gets out. If I hear anything, I will let you know at once."

Greig thanks her. He finishes his tea and accepts a packet of gingerbread to share with the members of his household. Then he and Lilith climb back up the stairs to the busy tearoom, where they bid each other a very fond farewell and Greig returns to the icy street.

Back at Scotland Yard, he makes arrangements with a team of constables for the snow-encrusted corpse to be transported from its location and placed upon the dissection table of Robertson, the police surgeon, in readiness for the causes of its mysterious demise to be revealed.

****

Detective Inspector Leo Stride of Scotland Yard's Detective Division is a man in dire need of an elsewhere to be. This is why he is currently making his way towards his place of employment, even though technically, he is still enjoying a well-earned Christmas break. The word 'enjoying' is not one that comes readily to mind, Stride thinks ruefully, as he picks a safe path gingerly along sludge encrusted pavements while at the same time avoiding the spray from passing carriages and carts.

There was food, yes. There was drink, in moderation. There were cards to line the mantelpiece. But there was also a never-ending stream of female friends and relatives of his wife. Numerous out-of-tune carol singers kept turning up, and a merry little band of local urchins played Knock Down Ginger every day with undiminished enthusiasm. Plus, his Christmas present from his life's companion consisted of a set of paintbrushes and a reminder that he had promised to paint the back kitchen in the New Year.

All in all therefore, it was with some relief that Stride received a letter from Lachlan Greig suggesting that he might like to return to work, as a rather perplexing case had turned up. Stride could have hugged the man. So now here he is, turning the corner into Covent Garden Piazza and smelling the fragrant aroma of coffee emanating from his favourite coffee stall outside Cox and Greenwood's.

Stride purchases a mug of his noxious tar-black brew and enters his place of work. He is a man in late middle age, with thinning hair and pouchy eyes. His suit is usually crumpled, but his mind is always razor-sharp and his face, as he mentally prepares himself for whatever he is about to encounter, wears an expression of almost beatific anticipation. He greets the desk constable fondly, then takes his mug of strong black coffee to Greig's office to find out what has happened to summon him so precipitously from the overstarched bosom of his family.

Having been briefed, Stride then prepares himself for the part of any inquiry that he personally most dislikes: a visit to the police morgue to view the victim of the crime. Robertson, the police surgeon, was educated at a top public school and then attended Oxford University before entering the medical profession.

Stride is a graduate of the 'school of hard knocks' and has worked his way up from there. He strongly suspects Robertson knows and takes great pleasure in making him feel intellectually inferior. Their relationship can best be described as hovering reluctantly on the borders of civility, which, added to Stride's almost pathological dislike of dead bodies, does not make for a happy confluence of minds.

Resignedly, he trails after Greig, steeling himself for what he is about to encounter.

****

"Ah, detective inspector, here you are at last!" Never has the greeting of Robertson fallen more plangently upon the ear, Stride thinks, as he and Greig enter the ice-cold mortuary together.

The plain, white-washed room is located across a courtyard from the main building. Windowless, its shelves are laden with bottles and glass-stoppered jars containing pickled objects of a bodily nature that he'd rather not think about.

At the centre of the room is the scrubbed table with its drainage outlets and the tools of the surgeon's trade: drills, surgical saws and knives. A stark reminder of what humanity is beneath the veneer of civilization: meat for worms. In deference to the winter weather, Robertson himself is wearing a check scarf and warm topcoat under his white apron. Black fingerless knitted gloves complete the outfit.

"I trust you have both participated in the various familial traditions of this festive season," Robertson continues, picking up a long, curved blade and studying it speculatively.

Stride has a sudden vision of Robertson at the head of some dining table, carefully dissecting (one couldn't possibly call it carving) a cooked turkey while treating his hapless guests to a history of its origins, its internal organs and various criminal cases concerning turkeys. He tries to banish the vision, but it lingers tantalizingly at the edges of his mind.

"And now, gentlemen, to our muttons, as our French friends say," Robertson continues, raising the black cloth covering the body with a flourish in a gesture reminiscent of a magician revealing the outcome of some magical trick. "What we have here, gentlemen, is a perfectly preserved corpse of a male. It is not often that the inclemency of the weather makes a positive contribution to the outcome of someone's demise, though I must say that death by cold is a rare phenomenon in this country. Death by cold and inanition combined is not unknown however, particularly in a severe winter such as we are currently enduring."

"So the man died from cold?" Stride says, fixing his gaze upon the opposite side of the room where there is an absence of corpses.

"Did I say that, detective inspector? I think I did not. I believe the actual words I uttered were a perfectly preserved corpse. And so he is. The appearance of the body ~ you observe the pallor of the skin, combined with dusky red patches are typical of the effects of cold, along with the stiffness in the muscles of the limbs and the face. However, detective inspector, it may well be that the actual cause of this man's demise lies elsewhere."

"Where does it lie then?" Stride exclaims recklessly, impatience, caffeine and the presence of a dead body getting the better of him.

Robertson, a raised eyebrow in human form, shoots him a steely glance. "There are also signs of starvation. The body is much emaciated. It appears from a very preliminary and cursory examination that the man has been deprived of nourishment over some period of time. Whether this is the result of deliberate action on his or another's part I am unable to say. I could refer you to the case of Mark Cornish who was killed by starvation and exposure by his father and stepmother. I could just as well refer you to several strange cases involving 'Fasting Girls' ~ where the individuals, all young, deliberately refused to partake of nourishment. I also note the general condition of the body, which indicates that the man has, in all likelihood, spent at least the latter part of his life as a street dweller.

"I have perused your report, Detective Inspector Greig, which I found thorough, as usual. You state that there was no evidence of blood on the ground, suggesting that the death of this person took place elsewhere and the body was transported to its final resting place, where it was encased in snow. Why, and for what purpose are matters outwith my bailiwick. I leave such speculation to your good selves."

"And his clothes?" Greig asks.

Robertson points to a neat pile of ragged grey garments. "I am afraid that, once thawed out, it appears that the man was clad in his small clothes only. You are welcome to take them with you. And, of course, the top hat. Meanwhile, I shall attempt to ascertain how precisely he met his unfortunate end, leaving the location and its significance to you. Until I have made further investigations, I shall, as usual, proceed with caution and reserve. My conclusions will be with you *pro tem*. Until then, I bid you both good day." He smiles at them in a complacent and self-satisfied manner.

"He is getting worse," Stride observes gloomily, as the two make their way back to the comparative warmth of the main building. "We shall need a translator soon."

Greig agrees. "Meanwhile, let us examine the top hat," he says. "With a bit of luck, it should provide us with some evidence to identify the dead man. Perhaps we might also have a description of him circulated to other police offices. I also think we ought to write to Mr. James Barrowclough and ask him to call into Scotland Yard at his earliest convenience. I'd like him to take a look at the body and see if he recognises the man."

"Good idea," Stride nods. "A human snowman. I must say, Lachlan, I think this is the most bizarre case I have come across in my whole career. And it has a lot of contenders: the curate's umbrella, the Clapham Common omnibus driver, and the missing Afghan diamond, to name but three." He scrapes the grey slush from his boots. "How I hate this weather. Backend of Christmas. New Year just creeping in. Cold, grey. Everything's dead."

"Including our mysterious snowman," Greig says thoughtfully. He turns the top hat over and examines the interior. "This was rather a fine hat once. Beaver, I think. Handmade, silk lining. Must have been expensive. Was our victim an office clerk, or someone above him socially who'd fallen on hard times? I can just make out the hatter's name: Lock & Co. of St James' Street. I think I will pay them a call and see what they have to say. Strike while the iron is hot."

A short while later, Detective Inspector Greig arrives outside 6 St James' Street, the location of the double fronted shop of Lock & Co. In one of the bow windows he spies a display of formal top hats of various heights and designs. The other window contains bowlers, soft hats, golf caps, hat boxes and the ingenious wooden head-measuring device that Greig remembers, from ordering his own top hat for his wedding, is called a *conformateur*.

He pauses, the sight of the object suddenly transferring him back into the past, to that glorious day when he finally made Miss Josephine King his wife. Not a day passes that Greig does not marvel at his good fortune. He'd admired her from afar for a long while. Then from a bit nearer, until gradually, he'd got over his fear of rejection and invited her to meet him at the Lily Lounge to take tea. Greig smiles as he remembers that first encounter ~ over the course of his professional life, he had apprehended many a hardened criminal without turning a hair, but he approached the tearoom with his heart thumping like a railway engine at the prospect.

And soon they will be blessed by a third member of the family. Truly, he thinks, as he enters the shop, his cup runneth over. Greig steps up to the counter, where he is greeted formally by a stout, balding man with greying side whiskers. He is wearing a cream shirt, black waistcoat, a short jacket, and dark woollen trousers.

"Good day sir," he says, rubbing soft white hands together. "John Lock, owner of this exclusive establishment at your service. I hope the season finds you well. How may I assist you today? A fine beaver hat? A recreational cap in handwoven Scottish tweed? Everything made to measure on the premises and of the finest quality."

Greig explains the reason for his visit, producing the top hat from a cloth bag and placing it on the wooden counter.

John Lock regards the top hat suspiciously. He does not attempt to pick it up. "So you say this is one of our hats? Indeed? And it was found on a dead body? Hmm. Seems unlikely. Hats from Lock & Co. are not usually associated with events concerning dead bodies and the police. Hats from Lock & Co. are worn by bankers, members of Parliament, professional gentlemen and suchlike."

"Your name is inside the hat, Mr. Lock," Greig says. "As you can see if you examine it. If you are able to tell me when it was made, and for whom, it would help Scotland Yard investigate the crime."

The man continues to stare at the top hat as if it were some alien object. "I can see that it has suffered some rough treatment since it left the shop," he says, frowning. "This is a handmade Radley ~ one of our most expensive hats."

"It has endured at least one night out in the open."

"More than that, I'd say, officer. This hat has not been brushed for a long time." Lock tuts, eyeing the offensive headgear with distaste. "Look at the state of it," he continues, his voice rising as he warms to his theme. "There is some green MOULD on the band! A top hat from Lock & Co. should never suffer such an indignity."

"As you say," Greig replies equably, wondering what sort of individual cares more for the fate of an object of headgear than the fate of the man who last wore it. "May I leave it with you? I expect you have sales ledgers you can consult?"

"Possibly."

"Shall we say Thursday, then? I shall call back on Thursday morning and see what you have discovered."

"As you wish, officer," Lock says, still eyeing the top hat with distaste.

"You have my card," Greig says. "If you discover anything before that, please notify me at once."

Detective Inspector Greig has barely left Lock & Co. to return to his place of work, when a man wearing a soft cap pulled down over his forehead, a bright muffler and a tastelessly loud tweed jacket, steps out of the shadow of an opposite doorway and saunters casually across road, coming to a halt outside the hatters. Glancing swiftly up and down the street, he opens the shop door, and steps inside. As the hatter steps forward to greet what he hopes will be his next customer (who might this time purchase a hat rather than deposit one), the man reaches into his coat pocket and produces a card.

"Morning, squire. Mr. Richard Dandy, chief reporter for *The Inquirer*. The newspaper that represents the Man in the Street. I see you have just had a visit from one of Scotland Yard's detectives. Care to share what the visit was about? Strictly between you, me and the doorpost of course? If it's a good story, I could make it worth your while. Bit of publicity never went amiss, eh?"

And Dandy leans across the counter, smiling his crocodilian smile.

****

James William Malin Barrowclough is not a man to allow the grass to grow under his feet (actually, as a land speculator, he would be more likely to replace it with bricks and mortar), so when he receives a letter at his office requesting his presence at Scotland Yard, he straightway puts on his hat and overcoat, informs his staff that he will be back in a short while, and steps out into the wintry streets.

Arriving at the police building, he is directed towards the Anxious Bench, where relatives wait for news of their completely innocent nearest and dearest who have been unjustly detained by the brutal and vicious police force for something they DID NOT DO, and they have the evidence to prove it. Whatever it was. On this occasion however, the bench is deserted, indignation requiring slightly more temperate conditions to manifest itself successfully.

Barrowclough uses the time to study the Wanted posters and the Police Help Needed notices. He wishes he had not hurried out without his gloves or muffler. The front office is as cold as the street outside. Eventually, just as he is about to approach the desk and launch into a 'my time is money' tirade, Detective Inspector Greig appears.

"Ah, Mr. Barrowclough, sir. Please excuse me for keeping you waiting. Sundry police matters," he says smoothly.

Barrowclough clears his throat. "Well, yes. I 'ave been waiting," he says crossly. Corrects it to 'have'. "Now then, officer, what is this about? I'm guessing it is something to do with that ... thing ... you found on my land ~ though how it can involve me is beyond my comprehension."

Greig ignores the dismissive comment. "I should like you to glance at some photographs of the dead man," he says. "It is just possible that he may be known to you. We are looking for the reasons why somebody would choose your grounds to leave him there."

"As I said from the outset: this prank, or whatever it was, has nothing whatsoever to do with me or my family and other than frightening my boys, I see no reason for it," Barrowclough replies testily.

"Nevertheless," Greig persists, not allowing his mask of reasonableness to slip for an instant. "If you would be so kind as to follow me to my office, I will show you the photographs."

Earlier, Greig has laid a series of photographs on his desk, ready for Barrowclough's arrival. They show the face of the corpse in various positions. Barrowclough studies them for a couple of seconds, in silence, then swallows hard.

"No, I do not recognise the face."

"You are sure, sir? The man was much emaciated when his body was thawed out. It is possible that his features might have looked differently in life."

"Perhaps so, but I never saw this man before. And now, officer, if that is all, you must excuse me; I have important work to return to. I hope you will not bother me or my family about this matter further. Is that quite understood?"

Barrowclough is shown out of Scotland Yard, leaving Greig to return and gather up the photographs. But he is not convinced by the man. Greig is sure that there is a connection. The person (or persons) unknown who deliberately left that body for the family to find, had their reasons for doing so. He does not yet know what the reasons are, or indeed who the individual is, but he is determined he is going to find out. With or without the help of the uncooperative Mr. Barrowclough.

****

After his encounter with the facial interior of the snowman, James Barrowclough experiences a distinct disinclination to return to work. Despite his assurances to the detective, he is disturbed by his visit to Scotland Yard. He feels in need of something restorative, something to take his mind off what he has just seen. After all, it is not every day that one encounters the images he has just had to view. What better than a visit to his club where refreshments and like-minded company are on offer?

Therefore, he directs his steps towards Piccadilly and, after a brisk walk, arrives outside a white-painted building with ornate pillars and a portico. He turns in at the door, where he is greeted respectfully by the porter. This is better. He didn't like the detective's manner. It lacked respect. He hands in his top hat, gloves and stick and mounts the stairs to the members' smoking room.

The Colossus Club, situated off Piccadilly, is not one of the top establishments such as the Athenaeum or the Garrick; its members err on the side of acquired money and aspirations rather than birth, in contrast to the more long-standing gentlemen's clubs, where ministers of the Crown, intellectuals and members of the aristocracy freely mix and mingle. But though of lesser status, it fulfils the same function: a place where similarly-minded individuals can go to talk, read the daily newspapers, eat big dinners and escape from their wives. It is widely considered that a chap without a club is like a hackney without a horse.

Arriving at his destination, Barrowclough scans the room to see who is 'in' on this cold crisp January morning. He is in luck: there is Dominic Jarvis, a man with dyed black moustaches and oiled hair, who always exudes the odour of strong pomade. His small, lidded eyes are closely set, giving the impression of a sly fox. Jarvis glances up from his copy of *The Daily Telegraph* as Barrowclough lowers his bulk into a nearby armchair and signals to the waiter to bring him a brandy and soda.

"Bit early in the day isn't it, old chap?" Jarvis observes.

"Not if you've just come from Scotland Yard like I have."

Jarvis raises a thin eyebrow. And waits. A balloon glass of brandy is placed on the small rosewood table by Barrowclough's elbow.

Barrowclough leans forward, lowering his voice. "There was a dead body on my land. The fellow had been made into a sort of snowman. I had to call in the police to take it away. Just been down to see if I recognised who it was."

"And did you?"

"No. Of course not. Probably some sort of practical joke, but nothing to do with me. And so I told them, good and straight."

Jarvis rattles the paper. "Nothing in here about it."

"Should hope not. Man's no longer master of his own property if any Tom, Dick or Harry can just break in and leave corpses lying around." He fixes Jarvis with a stern look. "And don't you go mentioning it to anybody else, understand?"

Jarvis shrugs. "As you wish. So, how is the little woman?" he asks, his face wiped of any expression.

Barrowclough shoots him a sharp look, but there is nothing to fasten upon. "Fine." He picks up a copy of another newspaper and pretends to peruse it. Silence falls. Eventually he downs the last of the brandy and soda, and lumbers to his feet. "Well, I'll be off. Time and tide, as they say."

Jarvis waves a hand casually, before burying his nose in his own newspaper once more. But behind the closely typed columns, he is smiling. He and Barrowclough have been business rivals for years. Ever since the younger man left his employ, taking a few of his more lucrative clients with him. Beneath the superficial bonhomie, there is little love lost between them. He regards the man as an upstart. Money but no class. And of course, there are rumours about the marriage too. But he has just been handed a juicy morsel of gossip, so he sits on, mulling it over, working out who he might tell and what they might do with the information.

****

Time passes. The snow is swept up by an army of street cleaners with spades, who clang and curse their way round the city, so that every main thoroughfare becomes lined by blue-white mountains. Small urchins revel in the opportunities afforded to slide down them, and hurl stones encased in snow at passers-by. 'Knock his hat off' is the name of the game and it is played with great glee. People venture out of their dwellings with slightly more confidence now they do not have to risk life and limb on the slippery footways. Life returns to some semblance of normality.

Here is the noonday coach from somewhere rattling through the streets, the horses tossing their heads and blowing out steam, their harness jingling. The passengers on top and outside are wrapped in furs, and travelling rugs, their faces purple with cold. The driver on the box blows a horn to warn people to clear out of the way, for he has a coaching inn to reach, and a warm fire and a hot toddy to enjoy.

Here is the same coach swinging under a brick archway and coming to a halt at the rear of the Old Bell in Holborn. It is one of the last coaching inns; the railways have taken away most of the trade. The coachman swings himself down, shouts the name of the inn and the city (because you never know, do you, there might be sone idiot who thinks he has arrived in Chelmsford), before barking orders to the inn's groom to feed and water the 'osses.

The steps are let down with a rattle and the passengers scramble or are helped to descend and head immediately for the warmth of the snug. Shorn of its passengers, the coach takes on the identity of some enormous toy, its bright claret livery splashed with mud. Look more closely: there is a sudden movement inside. A face rises to the side window. Next, the door is opened cautiously, and someone jumps down.

Peering all round cautiously, they check the yard is deserted. Then they stick two fingers into their mouth and give a shrill whistle. A second later, the lid of a great trunk attached to the rear of the coach lifts itself up slightly. Another figure emerges, swings its legs over the side of the trunk and slides down into the straw-covered mush of the yard.

"That was hard going, Flitch," it says, removing a cap and revealing itself to be a young girl with a pale peaky face surrounded by scattery brown curls. Her eyes are golden brown, long-lashed and luminously watchful, like a cat.

Flitch appears to be a wiry boy, a couple of years older. He has long, matted dark hair, prominent cheekbones and a world-weary expression. He is wearing a pair of trousers that are a size too short and a man's jacket that is a size too big. Both have seen better days but never participated in them.

"We did it though, Liza. We're here, in London. No more workhouse. No more beatings. No more overseer," he says.

"No more porridge and scrubbing," the girl agrees. "No more sewing and mangling." She pauses, clasping her chilled hands together, her eyes clouding. "No more Ma ..."

Her companion puts an arm round her shoulders. "You ain't going to think about that, Liza. Our Ma ~ she's with the angels now and that's a good place to be, innit? She's prob'ly looking down on us right now and giving a great big cheer that we got away. So let me go and get some grub. You'll feel better with a hot dinner inside you."

The boy called Flitch squares his shoulders and heads for the main entrance. The girl glances round the yard, then selects a quiet corner, where she squats down, lowers her breeches and relieves herself. Straightening up and buttoning the breeches, she saunters across to the horses, who are contentedly munching some hay. She pats their noses, then dips her hands into the bucket of drinking water, flinching at the cold, and splashes some water on her face and neck. The horses blow through their nostrils and continue eating.

The girl returns to the rear of the coach and pulls a small bundle from the trunk. As she does so, she spies the boy coming round the side of the inn. He is now wearing a kitchen apron and carrying two bowls that steam enticingly in the chill air.

"Got us some nice meat soup," he says, handing her one of the bowls.

The girl gulps down the welcoming broth, running a finger round the bowl to scoop up the last tasty remnants. "How've you done that, Flitch?" she asks, handing the bowl back and pointing at the apron.

He laughs. "Easy. I just went down to the kitchen. They're running around like scalded cats in there, trying to get all the dinner orders served. There's a big party of clerks in and they're banging on the tables for their food. So I helped myself to an apron I found on a chair, and pretended I was one of the scullery boys. Said I'd take a couple of bowls upstairs to the waiters in the bar. They was all so flustered, they just handed the bowls over, no questions asked."

Liza regards him with open admiration. "That was clever of you, Flitch."

The boy gives her a wry smile. "I been thinking, Liza. Best we don't let on where we come from. If people found out we escaped from the workhouse, they'd try to send us back. If anybody asks, we are just a brother and sister, minding our own business. Like back then, before we was turned out of the cottage and sent to that place. Agreed?"

"Agreed," the girl nods, though 'before' barely exists anymore in her mind. The before of skylarks and blue skies, flowers and green fields. Before has been unremembered. It has slipped through the cracks of time, to where all the lost things go.

"We have our own bowls now," the boy tells her. "And an apron we can sell. And I found some money in a pocket. Not much, but enough for lodgings for the night." He grins conspiratorially, before swinging himself up onto the roof of the coach, where he helps himself to one of the fur travelling rugs. Clambering down, he ties it round his shoulders, bandolier style. "Right, let's be off, before anybody catches us."

"Be off where?"

The boy stretches both arms in an expansive gesture. "Wherever we like. We got a whole city to choose from, Liza. And all the time in the world to explore it. There's bound to be rich pickings somewhere." He holds out his hand. "C'mon, let's go and have an adventure."

****

As Flitch and his fellow escapee set out on their new life, a short distance away, Detective Inspector Stride is flicking through the lunchtime editions of the newspapers, which have just been set out on his desk by one of the constables.

Stride pages idly through the usual unlikely fictions that fill the column inches when there is nothing happening newsworthy enough to fill them. Frozen fountains, gigantic icicles, carts upturned, colder winters, milder winters. He is surprised somebody hasn't reported the appearance of an Ice Age dinosaur, lumbering along Oxford Street.

All at once, Stride stiffens. His eyes focus in on an article on page three of *The Inquirer*. After a few seconds of intense study, Stride rises, goes to the door and bellows out an order. His cry is answered by the sound of boots in the corridor.

"Get Greig!" he commands when a fresh-faced constable appears.

"Sir, yes sir, at once," babbles the youth. The boots pound into the distance, shortly replaced by the even tread of Detective Inspector Greig, who enters the office, eyebrows raised quizzically.

"Have you seen this?" Stride demands, thrusting the folded-back newspaper across the desk. "Not only has that waste of space Richard Dandy ~ who has the nerve to call himself a journalist ~ written a load of utter speculative rubbish about the man you found encased in snow, 'Mr. No-Man' he calls him, but apparently members of the public can now view the 'Murderer's Top Hat' at Lock & Co.'s exclusive hat emporium for the bargain price of 2d."

Greig pulls a face. "Oh dear. Most unfortunate."

"Indeed. As you correctly say. Most. I warn you, as soon as these penny-a-liner hacks come up with some ridiculous nickname, we are fighting a losing battle. The man in the street decides not to take it seriously. 'Mr. No-Man. Murderer's Top Hat'! Next thing, we'll have mockery, ridicule and nobody will offer us any vital information. I have a good mind to go straight round to *The Inquirer's* office and demand the editor withdraw the article!"

"Possibly too late," Greig says. "However, Mr. Lock will not be able to display the hat for much longer, as I intend to relieve him of it this morning. Hopefully with the name of the original owner."

Twenty minutes later, and armed with a bag, Greig leaves Scotland Yard and heads for St James' Street and the hapless hatter. He arrives at the shop to find a small crowd gathered outside it, muttering crossly to itself. There is the sound of fists hammering from the side of the crowd nearest to the shop door.

"What has happened here?" Greig inquires.

"Bin a break-in," a large grubby-aproned woman informs him.

"We walked all the way from Poplar to look at the Murderer's Top Hat like it said in the paper, and now we can't. Disgraceful, I calls it," a man says. Two small children cling to his coat tails, their faces blue with cold and sullen with disappointment.

Greig pushes his way through. A workman is securing wooden boards to one of the windows, where it appears the glass has been smashed. He skirts round him, and knocks on the shop door, which has a 'closed' sign. After a few more knocks, Lock appears from the rear of the shop, recognises him and opens the door. The crowd surges forward. Lock leans against the door and turns the key. The crowd press their faces to the unshattered glass and gesticulate.

"Ah, officer. Yes. It's Thursday, isn't it? You'd better come through to the back," the hatter sighs. He gestures towards the window. "It has been like this all morning."

Greig follows him to the workroom at the rear, where a group of employees sit at a long table. Some are stitching ribbon and bias binding bands round hats of various styles. Some more are laying out patterns and cutting flat caps under the watchful eye of an overseer. The shelves on the four walls are crammed with rolls of woollen cloth, pelts, coloured silk, jars of paste and starch, and the ubiquitous conformateurs. In one corner, a number of dinner baskets are piled up. There is a strong smell of glue. As the two men enter, every worker pauses, glances up, then hastily bends over their work. An invisible air of 'listening but not listening' begins to form.

Lock invites Greig to take a seat. Greig sits and waits, placing the cloth bag pointedly on his knees. Lock remains standing. He clears his throat, starts rocking gently on his heels, inserts his thumbs into his waistcoat pockets. Greig continues waiting. He is pretty sure he knows exactly what has happened, but he is not going to throw the man a lifeline. Two of the workers exchange a meaningful glance behind the hatter's back.

"You see, officer, it's like this," Lock says finally, his voice lowered. "I arrived at the shop this morning to find there'd been a break-in. Someone had forced the shutters and smashed the window,"

"Most lamentable," Greig says. He goes on waiting.

"It appears that whoever broke into the shop got away with the day's takings and ..." Locke swallows, "the top hat that you left with me. I have made a thorough examination of the premises, but I cannot find it anywhere."

There is a long pause.

"I see," Greig says at last.

Locke wrings his hands. "I am so sorry, officer. I cannot think how such a thing could happen."

More silence.

"Perhaps allowing members of the press to write articles in the newspapers advertising its presence might have contributed?" Greig suggests drily.

Lock starts. "Oh, do you think that was the reason?"

A ripple of amusement runs round the table. He glares at the workers. They bend their heads over their work once more.

"I can only offer my profound and deepest apologies, officer," Lock says, unctuously. "From my examination of the top hat prior to its disappearance, I have to say it was in a pretty poor state of repair. It obviously suffered much neglect since it left my emporium. But I have managed to find the name of the original owner for you." He smiles brightly, in a hopeful manner. "Here it is. I have been carrying it in my pocket, all ready to hand over to you."

Greig unfolds the piece of paper and reads the name. He reads it again. Two small frown lines appear between his brows.

"Of course, if the top hat turns up at any future time, I shall let you know, officer," Lock says, his fixed grin hanging onto the edges of his face by its fingertips. "At once, officer," he adds, his grin now at rictus level.

Greig nods perfunctorily. "There is a back way out of this shop, I presume. I do not wish to run the gamut of that crowd."

"Yes, of course. If you would kindly follow me," Locke gurns.

Greig tucks the pieces of paper into his overcoat pocket and follows the hopeless hatter out of the workroom and into a dingy back alley. He makes his way to the street and sets off determinedly back to Scotland Yard. This is a development he has not anticipated. He needs to cogitate upon its significance.

****

While Inspector Greig is walking and contemplating, let us turn our focus elsewhere. Behold the wonder that is Regent Street, the finest street in town, with the finest shopfronts to match! Here are the great department stores, all plate glass, electric lighting and magnificence: Swan and Edgar, Peter Robinson and Dickens and Jones, to name but a few. London's West End boasts the largest and smartest shops in the country, crammed full of furniture, articles of household wares, fashion, in fact everything the modern man or woman could desire, arranged artistically to entice them inside and thence persuade them to part with their money.

Here are the carriages of the wealthy, all gloss and lacquered woodwork, parked in a long line outside the department stores, awaiting their owners' return. Liveried footmen stamp their cold feet or warm their chapped fingers round a cup of something hot. Nobody takes any notice of the boy and girl making their way along the snow-pasted pavement, their eyes big as saucers as they stare into each delightful shop window, marvelling at so much wonderful stuff. To the affluent shoppers, they are just street detritus, to be brushed aside as they saunter along.

Since we last encountered them, Liza has undergone a makeover, in that the stolen items have been exchanged for a second-hand dress in a colour best described as dead rat and a dilapidated bonnet in crushed black velvet. Flitch however, is still dressed in the clothes he arrived in ~ there is only so much you can get out of a second-hand apron and two bowls.

As the two feast their eyes on the bright fruits displayed in wooden boxes outside a greengrocer's shop, their mouths watering, there is a sudden shout. A small white fluffy dog has escaped from inside one of the carriages, where it was awaiting its owner's return. Two coachmen give chase. Barking defiantly, the dog darts between their legs and scurries along the pavement towards the two youngsters.

Liza squats down and holds out her hand. The dog pauses, regarding her speculatively out of its little black eyes. With her other hand, she extracts a small piece of stale bread from the pocket of her dress. "Here you are, nice little doggie ~ want some food?" The dog trots over and sniffs the bread. Liza picks it up, snuggling her cold face into its warm fur. The dog licks her cheek.

Next minute, a heavy gloved hand descends upon her shoulder and a loud voice yells, "Oi, you! Street scum! I saw you! Trying to steal Precious Petal? I know your game!"

One of the coachmen has Liza in his grasp. She struggles, protesting her innocence. The small dog barks furiously and tries to bite the man's hand. A crowd gathers (of course it does). The state of Liza's clothes is commented upon, this being reason enough to brand her a thief and a criminal. The coachman hangs onto her shoulder, his fingers gripping it tightly. Liza squirms, trying to free herself. The dog snarls and snaps at the man.

The impasse is eventually broken by a large woman swathed in furs, who pushes her way through the crowd. "What on earth is happening?" she exclaims in a loud plummy voice. "I left Precious Petal in the coach. You were supposed to be looking after her."

The burly coachman turns to face her, his fingers still digging cruelly into Liza's shoulder. "This filthy beggar girl stole the dog out of the coach, madam. I have apprehended her in the very act of trying to make off with it. I suggest you call the police and have her arrested for theft."

Liza goes on protesting her innocence, but nobody is listening. The crowd is now divided between the rights of pet owners to take their animals wherever they wish, and the rights of individuals not to have their belongings stolen from under their noses. Personal anecdotes are shared. And then a constable arrives. The crowd parts and miraculously melts away.

"Now then, what's going on here?" the constable inquires.

The coachman and the fur-clad woman both attempt to present their side of the story at the same time. Liza still holds the small dog, who is now shaking and whimpering in her arms. She says nothing. Long incarceration in the workhouse has taught her that silence is the best response to practically anything. At which point, an imposing middle-aged woman in a tailored navy woollen coat and matching navy bonnet approaches the little group. She carries a wicker basket over one arm.

"Excuse me, constable, but I witnessed the whole thing," she says. Her voice is low but has a ring of authority. "I was just coming out of Peter Robinson, where I have been conducting business with the catering manager. I saw this man chatting to some other coachmen. He was not paying the slightest attention to the carriage, and so did not see the dog climbing out of the side window. The young girl managed to catch the dog before it plunged into the road, where it would undoubtably have perished under the wheels of a passing vehicle. Far from being a thief, she rescued it, and should be rewarded for her efforts. That is all."

The woman smiles encouragingly at Liza, who ventures a small, cautious smile in return. Then she holds out the dog to the constable, who hands it over in turn to its rightful owner.

"And the reward?" the woman says pointedly, looking at the fur-clad one.

Rolling her eyes, the woman nods at the coachman. "Pay the girl."

Reluctantly, the coachman gives Liza a couple of coins.

"As it was your fault, her reward can come from your wages. And I shall be having a word with your master when we get home," the fur-clad one says, as she and the dog are ladled back into the coach. The dog instantly presses its small nose to the window and stares out at Liza, as if trying to imprint her face upon its memory. The coachman unwinds the reins from the whipstock, cracks his whip and the pair of matching bays set off at a smart trot in the direction of Regent Circus.

"Well, you was lucky there, my gal," the constable says. "That could've gone very badly for you. Now, be on your way and think yourself fortunate."

Liza glances all around, but her rescuer is nowhere to be seen. Instead, Flitch detaches himself from a neighbouring doorway and saunters over. "How much you got, Liza?"

The girl shows him. Flitch whistles. "Whew! Enough for a couple of good beds tonight and a nice fish supper.

Maybe even some boots." He digs in his jacket pocket. "And look what I have ~ two apples." He hands one over. "S'funny what suddenly falls out of a fruit box, innit?" he grins.

Munching their apples, they set off together along the dirty pavement. "This has been a good day," Flitch says as they head in the direction of Tottenham Court Road. "And tomorrow will be even better. You wait and see."

$$****$$

Sadly, the day is not turning out to be even better for Detective Inspector Stride. When Greig returns to Scotland Yard, he finds his colleague reading through Robertson's autopsy report while fortifying himself with swigs of bitter-black coffee from a stained china cup.

"Just as I thought," Stride says. "The poor man died of cold and want after living on the street for some time. Nothing in his stomach. Though why it takes Robertson three pages to come to the same conclusion is beyond me."

"There will have to be a coroner's inquest," Greig says.

"If we can find someone to hold it. The Middlesex coroner is snowed up somewhere in Yorkshire. Left London before Christmas and hasn't returned since, I gather. No trains, apparently. No coaches either. Barbaric place, Yorkshire." Stride glances up and catches the edge of Greig's expression. "But you are looking quizzical. And it can't be on account of this report, because you haven't had the misfortune of reading it. Unlike me."

"I have just returned from Lock & Co.," Greig tells him. "It appears there was a burglary last night and the top hat I left there has been taken."

Stride makes a face. "I am guessing its theft can be traced directly back to *The Inquirer*."

"However, the hatter has been able to trace the man who bought it originally," Greig continues, drawing the piece of paper from his pocket. "Here is his name," he says, placing the paper on the desk.

Stride picks up the paper and reads the name. He gives a low whistle. "Now that is not what I expected. Not at all. Throws a very interesting light on matters, does it not?"

"Indeed," Greig says. "I think I shall write and request a meeting. I won't enlighten him as to the reason why I am writing, of course. And I was also wondering whether to brief Detective Constable Williams. I'd like to have him with me on this case."

Stride drums a pencil against the side of his cup. "Ah yes. Good idea. Now young Williams has been accepted into the detective division, we should use him. We don't want him applying to another police office because he feels unappreciated."

Greig nods his agreement, not admitting that the reason he wants to share the investigation is the thought of his wife and her advanced pregnancy. A second detective will halve the work, and more importantly, the paperwork. Right now, he'd like to see his home a little more and his Scotland Yard office a little less.

"Then with your permission, I shall go and explain the matter to him at once," he says, rising from his seat. "And as soon as I have done so, I will write my letter. We must seize time firmly by the forelock, as my Scottish grandmother used to say." He gives Stride a disarming grin and goes, leaving Stride to mull over his remark, and then puzzle his way through the bewildering complexities of the police surgeon's report once more.

****

Meanwhile, the weather is still causing havoc in the city streets, not helped by the onward march of the railways. Whole areas are subject to clearance; excavations topple buildings and render others structurally precarious, having to be supported by huge pieces of timber. The crush and crowding of the streets are made worse by yawning chasms, only traversable by planks. The *bouleversement* of London is everywhere: a row of ancient tenements dating back to Elizabethan times are here today, gone tomorrow. A shop that sold groceries is now boarded up, its owner moved elsewhere. A street of terraced houses falls like a row of dominoes.

And always the mechanical sounds of drilling, hammering, digging, and the crash of falling masonry as the underground railway bores its way through structures that have withstood the ravages of time, but cannot stand before the workmen's tools. While, beneath the teeming and despoiled metropolis, dark tunnels wait the trainloads of passengers, who will experience the disorientation and dislocation of travelling underneath the chaotic city above their heads.

All this change and improvement is not going unremarked. Indeed, it is being closely studied by a small group of artists. Called the Transformative Brotherhood, they rent a decrepit terrace house in a back alley off Camden High Street. Their focus is the London Street: the architecture (which can be sold to the fashionable papers), construction and destruction (*The Illustrated London News* has full page engravings) and scenes of incidents, street people and their living conditions.

Not for these artists paintings of languorous long-haired white-faced damsels in shapeless frocks, waving lilies in their wan hands or floating face-up in baths pretending to be Shakespearean heroines. Down with dilettantes! Eschew effetes! These artists are portraying the grit and grime of changing London ~ which is why their streetwear consists of workmen's overalls, stout boots, tweed jackets and flat caps, causing them to be frequently mistaken for house painters to which the response is always: "Dear madam/sir I am an ARTIST, not a decorator".

Today, Walter Hugo Hunter, graduate of the Royal Academy, is patrolling the excavations at the Holborn Valley Viaduct, the great raised roadway being built to help people and traffic traverse the steep ascent along Holborn Hill and link the commercial life of the West End with the banking district of the city. Hunter has already submitted a detailed pen and ink drawing of the works to *The London Illustrated News* showing the massive destruction of daily life during the two years of construction.

Now he has returned, this time seeking inspiration on a smaller, more human scale. The snow has all but vanished, and the air is crisp, with smoke blowing into a granite sky, and loud with the clang of hammers. Hunter is looking for something different to the conventional street scenes, the anodyne and conventional. He wants to disturb, to shock. He takes up his position close to the ornamental Gothic-style cast-iron bridge and surveys the area.

There are plenty of well-dressed Londoners viewing the final touches from the safety of a raised platform, guarded by police constables. But no, they are not inspiring him today. Nor are the gangs of navvies, and the surveyors with their plans and surveying instruments.

But look, over there ~ by a gap in the hoardings ~ two small figures. Two wretched beggar children. Aha ~ that is more like it! Hunter hurries down the temporary wooden stairs leading to the road beneath. Here is his next composition: the massive street construction rising out of the ground like a colossus, dwarfing the tiny, insignificant mendicants scratching a precarious living at its feet.

As he draws closer, Hunter sees that the two figures are in reality a girl and a boy. And not as mendicant as he had first thought. Their clothes are ill-fitting but appear reasonably clean. He notices, sadly, that they both have boots. Damn. He will have to improvise: the figures in the painting must be bare-foot and ragged for the contrast to be truly effective.

Hunter greets them. The boy and girl turn and look at him, cautiously. The boy, he observes, has the nascent and unformed features of one on the cusp of manhood. The girl wears a too-large, dilapidated bonnet of some worn velvet material, but under it, her skin is dusted with freckles and her eyes are quite startling ~ brown, the irises splattered with golden lights deep down in the black. The eyes of a tiger he saw recently at the Zoological Gardens. The girl's lashes curl up like insect legs. Astonishing. Yes. She will make a wonderful subject.

He elicits their names, then explains carefully what he wants of them, getting his sketchbook and chalks from the leather satchel he carries over his shoulder. He shows them some of his work. They regard his drawings in fascinated silence. Eventually the boy speaks. "You want to draw me and Liza? Fine ~ but it'll cost."

Hunter is amused by his boldness. "I see, my fine young fellow. And what sum do you have in mind?"

The boy beckons to the girl, and they go into a huddle. After a brief discussion, he returns. "Half crown."

"You strike a hard bargain."

"Each. What do you want us to do?"

Hunter positions them by one of the hoardings. It is covered with torn advertisements, a few from Christian charities reminding people of their duty to succour the poor. He makes the girl crouch down, her back against the hoarding, hands round her knees in a pose suggesting abject poverty. She looks up pleadingly. The boy stands next to her, looking down, pity on his face. Once they are both in position, and after ordering them to stay as still as possible, he starts sketching.

Time passes. Hunter throws down one sketch after another. This is going to be a masterpiece. Two young waifs in the foreground, starving and homeless, advertisements promoting Christian charity and Bourneville cocoa, and behind them, the iron-grey structures of the nearly completed viaduct reaching up into a grey pitiless sky. A stark and pointed commentary on the state of modern industrial society.

Eventually, Hunter indicates to his two models that they can relax. He closes the sketch book and replaces it in his satchel, from which he now draws a packet of beef sandwiches. Alice Mor (maker of sculptures and meals ~ because gender equality doesn't change much, even in advanced artistic circles) has put him up a nice luncheon.

The youngsters swing their arms and stamp their feet. The boy gets out a pack of playing cards and starts shuffling them at amazing speed. Hunter unwraps the packet of food. The boy's hands still. Two pairs of eyes fix themselves upon the contents. Sighing, he beckons his young artist's models over and shares his meal. The youngsters wolf down the food as if they were starving, which, upon reflection, Hunter thinks they may well be.

Once the last crumb has been consumed, Hunter flicks through the sketchbook, checking that he has enough to lay down the preliminary lines of his painting. "I may need you both to pose for me again," he says. "Do you live around here? How may I find you?"

The boy grins. "We don't live here, mister. We're what you might call visiting. Ain't that so, Liza?"

The girl nods.

"I would be willing to pay you to pose for me again," Hunter says.

The girl and her companion eye each other, weighing up the offer. Hunter digs in his coat pocket, produces two half crowns and his card. "Here is the money for today, and here is my address. I shall start the painting when I get home. In two days' time, if you come in the morning, I promise to pay you again. And there will be food," he adds, "as an incentive."

The boy takes the money and the card. "Thanks mister. Now, I ain't saying we will come, understand. We might, we might not. Tomorrow, we could be somewhere else, who knows ~ wherever the adventure takes us."

Hunter is amused. "Well, either way, thank you very much for posing for me today. It is going to be a fine painting when it is done." He makes them a small, elegant bow before heading off towards the West End.

Flitch stares down at the two silver coins in his palm. "I thought I was going to have to play Find the Lady to get us some money. Now we've got enough for a lovely supper, beds and maybe a visit to the Music Hall tonight ~ I fancy a good singsong," he says.

Liza runs an index finger under the name on the card, her brow furrowed. "Wa ... l ... ter ... Hu ... n ... ter," she spells out laboriously.

Flitch's eyes widen in astonishment. "Cor, Liza, I never knew you could READ!"

The girl looks pleased with herself. "Granny Wickens taught me my letters in the workhouse. I ain't very good, but I can do it if I go slow and careful like." She tucks the visiting card away in a pocket. "He was a nice young man, Flitch. He gave us sandwiches, and money. And I'd like to see a painting of me."

"Then you shall, Liza," the boy says grandly. "Anything you want. You keep the card safe, and we'll do what he asks."

****

And so, a couple of days later, as Alice Mor, sculptress in residence, and wife of Charlie Mor, youngest scion of Lord Felix Mor, whose allowance is funding the Transformative Brotherhood (inadequately), is poking a lump of dough on the table in the basement kitchen, which also doubles as her studio and is currently the warmest room in the house, she becomes aware of two pairs of eyes regarding her curiously from the ground floor window.

The eyes vanish. Then she hears boots coming down the area steps and stopping on the other side of the blue kitchen door. There is a pause, then knocking. Alice Mor stretches her aching back, wipes her hands on her apron and goes to see who is there, mentally rehearsing her excuses if the visitors should be from one of the neighbourhood suppliers of provender.

It is a problem. The Transformative Brotherhood are extremely proficient at producing paintings, drawings and sculptures that do not sell at a price that covers their cost of living. Which means they are constantly in debt to the local butcher, baker and candlestick maker. You cannot make art on an empty stomach and standing for hours on end in the open-air sketching demolished buildings, or street scenes generates a healthy appetite. But pretty soon, the group are convinced, the art-buying public ~ which is overwhelmingly male, will tire of canvases depicting luscious females clad in flimsy gauze draped on sofas in provocative poses or rustic scenes with runny skies.

With this in mind, therefore, the other members of the Brotherhood are currently out seeing a man about a gallery space in the West End. It is time to show the great British public what they should be hanging on their walls. Their departure leaves Alice Mor in charge of providing the daily bread, which is what she is doing, albeit reluctantly, when Flitch and Liza show up at the kitchen door.

Alice Mor stares at the two young people. She does not recognise them as coming from any of the local shops. They carry no baskets, nor hold any envelopes or account books that she can see. She regards them quizzically, head on one side and waits to be enlightened. Flitch steps forward. He smiles confidently.

"Morning, miss. We're here to see our painting. Mr. Hunter the artist told us to come."

Light dawns. Alice Mor steps aside and allows them to enter kitchen. Two noses sniff the aroma appreciatively. She explains the situation, offers the suggestion of coming back later. But the kitchen is warm and fragrant, and the streets are cold and slushy, so by the time she has ended her speech, both young people are seated at the table, watching her expectantly.

"We can wait, miss," Flitch says. "We got nowhere else to be right now, have we Liza?"

The girl agrees. She observes Alice Mor poking the dough around in a disconsolate fashion. A memory returns. Sunshine on a flagged floor. Hens wandering in and out. Another kitchen table scrubbed clean. Hands working the dough on a floured wooden board. Her mother singing softly as she worked. "You want to give it a good push, miss. And fold it over. Heel and hand. That's how to make it rise," she suggests.

Alice Mor raises her eyes from the sticky mound of dough and stares wonderingly into the girl's face. "You know how to make bread? Really?"

Liza nods. Because suddenly she does. She has watched the process so many times. Only in the succeeding tragedy that took them out of the bright kitchen and into the bleak greyness of the workhouse, she forgot she knew. She gets up. "Here, let me help you," she says, wiping her hands on her dress.

By the time the rest of the Brotherhood return, loud and self-congratulatory after securing a gallery space in one of the new department stores, there are three loaves proving under dishcloths on top of the stove, and Alice, Flitch and Liza are sharing cups of hot sweet tea and anecdotes around the table.

After conveying the joyful news, Hunter takes his two models up to his studio on the second floor, where the painting is sitting on an easel. He positions them by the window, in their former poses and then begins to throw paint onto the canvas with alarming speed.

By the time Flitch and Liza leave the house, the street is filling with homecoming workers. The two youngsters follow the flow of people, letting themselves be taken wherever they are led. Flitch carries half a loaf of newly baked bread under his arm. His pocket chinks with coins. Liza has a warm blue knitted shawl with woolly tassels tied around her shoulders, a gift from Alice Mor. It has a few moth holes, but she doesn't care.

"Will we go and see the paintings?" she asks. "I've never seen a picture of me hung on a wall before."

"If we are still here," Flitch says.

"We're doing alright, aren't we, Flitch?" Liza says. "We've got supper, and some money and we was in the warm all day. And they said to come back anytime."

Flitch grins at her. "I told you, didn't I? Said we'd have a great adventure. And we are having one. Now let's find somewhere out of the cold to eat this good bread you made, and then we'll doss down for the night. Who knows what tomorrow will bring?"

****

For the Detective Division at Scotland Yard, tomorrow brings two constables down with heavy colds and a detective constable with food poisoning. Unfortunately, the detective constable is young Tom Williams, which means that Greig sets out unaccompanied to attend the scheduled meeting with the former owner of the top hat. It is not taking place where he was anticipating it, his letter having unexpectedly elicited a formal response from Barrowclough's lawyer and an invitation to attend him at his Chambers.

The Inns of Court consist of broad open squares, paved and generally treeless, surrounded by grubby mansions as large and cheerless as barracks. There are no entrance doors here, just a string of names painted in stripes on the doorposts. On your way to your destination, you may walk past a dingy barber's shop, with its dusty display of powdered wigs the same dirty white colour as the London snow, some small fruiterers offering withered apples, wrinkly oranges, damp biscuits, ginger beer and sandwiches for the refreshment of those attending the various courts. There are also law stationers, their windows covered with advertisements for clerkships wanted.

Greig walks under an archway, avoiding a small group of lawyers' clerks hurrying in the opposite direction towards the Law Courts, their hands full of red-tape-tied papers. He crosses a tiny backyard-like square, with one lanky-looking lamp post, ducks down a desolate back alley, and finally reaches the offices of Snare, Grip & Tightly, solicitors. After enquiring of the clerk, he is shown into the office of Lawyer Snare, a wizened beaky-nosed man with parchment-coloured skin and ink-stained fingers. He is clad in fusty black. The person Greig was expecting to interview is not present.

An inky claw waves the detective inspector to a chair, then opens a buff file on the desk. Perching a pair of glasses on the swooping beak, Lawyer Snare clears his throat. "Now then, detective. I am instructed by my client, Mr. James Barrowclough of Hill House, Hampstead, to inquire why and for what reason you wish to see him? My client has, I believe, already endured two most unpleasant interrogations at the hands of the Metropolitan Police, despite having nothing to do with the matter you write about.

"My client has also been the subject of articles in various daily newspapers, resulting in members of the public turning up at his gate and shouting inappropriate remarks. My client is therefore considering ~ and considering most carefully, whether, on the balance of probability, to bring charges against yourself and the organisation you represent for wilfully pursuing him for a crime he did not commit and the resultant harassment he and his family now endure. I use the word 'pursuing', I might also use the word 'persecuting'. What answer ye to the charge?"

Greig feels his anger rising. "I am attempting to discover why a homeless man was discovered dead on your client's estate. If your client thinks this has nothing to do with him, then he may be right. Alternatively, he may not. But impeding or attempting to subvert the course of an investigation is also a crime. Perhaps you could inform your client? Regardless, I shall continue to pursue my investigation. Your client will now be required, under caution, to attend Scotland Yard to answer certain questions that have arisen in the course of my investigation. Failure to do so may result in consequences that he probably would not wish to see enacted." Greig stands. "Tomorrow morning. Ten o'clock. Please convey my request to your client. Good day to you."

Greig returns to Scotland Yard, his anger unabated by the walk. The building is cold, the fire in his office a spluttering inadequacy. He opens the Barrowclough file (he refuses to call it the Snowman file) and writes up the notes from his meeting with the man's lawyer. Then he sits back and allows his thoughts to take him where they will. They lead him down a short path where a man dies of cold and want. He is placed in a particular location that seems to be significant. He wears a top hat belonging to the owner of the location.

The facts by themselves do not infer that a crime has been committed. Many hundreds of people die of cold and want every day in the richest city on the globe, particularly during the harsh winter months. They pass from this world to the next with few to mourn their departure. But somebody wants the death of this man to be noticed. His demise is significant. For reasons Greig does not yet understand.

Somebody is sending a clear message to Mr. James William Malin Barrowclough. Perhaps Greig might have been prepared to let matters lie before his meeting with the lawyer. Now, he has changed his mind. The man's reluctance to cooperate is sending up a red flag. There is a mystery here, and he is more than ever determined to get to the bottom of it.

Meanwhile, over in Hampstead, a small parcel is delivered to Hill House. It is taken in by one of the male servants, and placed on the hall table, to await the arrival of the master of the house. The servants know better than to handle or open any post addressed to Barrowclough, his wife or either of the two boys.

The daily routines of the household tick relentlessly on. Mantels are dusted. Rugs beaten. Floors are swept and polished. The two boys tramp in and out. Floors are polished again. Meals are served ~ the elderly nurse presides over the two boys, who deeply resent her presence but know they risk the wrath of their father if any report of bad behaviour reaches him. Nurse looked after their mother while she was growing up in this house, and although she is now half-blind, slightly illogical in her pronouncements and walks with a stick, they have been instructed to obey her implicitly or get a beating.

Upstairs, Helena Barrowclough lies in bed in a darkened room. Broth and assorted delicacies are brought to her at intervals by her personal maid. In the afternoon, the doctor visits, checks her pulse, and suggests opening the curtains. He recommends that she might like to sit by the window for a while. With a book, or some pleasant pastime.

It is three years since Helena took to her bed, plagued with headaches and palpitations. Her diagnosis varies, depending upon which doctor of the many consulted attends her. The current one belongs to the 'fresh air and diversions' school of thought. She preferred the one who said she should go abroad for the winter, but after a heated discussion with her husband on the landing, which she overhead, he has never come back.

The clock in the hallway chimes six, followed by the chimes of various other clocks. There is the sound of carriage wheels in the driveway. Then the front door opens, and masculine voices filter up from the hallway. It sounds as if James is cross about something. She sighs, a delicate zephyr of an outward breath. Hopefully, he will go straight to his study and help himself to a drink before looking in on her. She begins to arrange in her mind what she will say when he knocks on her bedroom door and prays that cook has prepared something tasty for his dinner. So much depends upon these small things.

While she awaits the outcome, Helena combs her hair with her fingers and re-ties her bedgown at the throat. She thinks about her room, which used to be her room when she was growing up in the house which itself was part of her marriage settlement. It is now her room once again, since she removed herself back to it at the outset of her unfortunate illness. Now, when she looks back from herself today to herself then, there is an almost unbroken line from the shining girl with all her hopes before her, to the invalid that she has turned into. As if everything in between happened to someone else.

She thinks about her husband and her two sons, who exist beyond the door of her sanctuary. It is so much easier to love them when they are not around. At a distance, all the blemishes and imperfections can be smoothed away. In person, she finds them loud, intrusive and intimidating. The boys in particular. Their energy exhausts her. It is like being in the presence of a pair of clumsy young carthorses. They also appear to be growing up in the exact image of their father. More's the pity. She would have liked to have had a girl, a small docile one she could train and who would be a companion to her. Too late now.

There is a discreet knock on her door: she recognises it as belonging to one of the housemaids. She voices her acknowledgement. The door opens. A tray of supper is brought in and placed on a side table by the bed. Some boiled whitefish, a glass dish of junket, a small glass of port. She has little appetite nowadays but sits herself up and prepares to do battle with her meal.

"How is Mr. Barrowclough?" she inquires as she forks the fish around listlessly.

The housemaid bites her lower lip. She is a recent acquisition to Hill House and has yet to be inducted into what she can and cannot mention upstairs. She is also a great reader, principally of crime thrillers and sensational novels and has benefited from an education, albeit a limited one.

"He received another of those parcels today, madam," she says, nodding in a significant fashion.

Helena Barrowclough sets down her fork. Slowly. "Yes?" she says in a go-on tone.

"That's all I know, madam. It was wrapped in brown paper. Like the previous one. He took it into his study straightaway as soon as he came home."

"Yes, I see. Thank you." The fork is picked up. A morsel of fish is conveyed vertically. "Well, Marian, isn't it? I shall ring when I am ready for you to remove the tray."

Dismissed, the housemaid scurries back down to the safety of the kitchen regions, where her fellow servants are busily preparing the evening meal for the remaining members of the Barrowclough family. She is given a tray of cutlery and instructed to go and lay the table in the dining room and make sure all the silver knives and forks are absolutely straight and that the two boys have their special water glasses.

On her way, the newish housemaid passes the master's study. She pauses outside the door. A rhythmic sound can be heard, as if someone is kicking the desk. It is accompanied by furious exclamations. The housemaid listens for a while, then goes about her task. There is definitely something strange going on, she thinks to herself. Tomorrow, while the family are still asleep in their various bedrooms, she decides she might take a soft cloth into the master's study. His desk could do with a bit of a polish.

The morrow arrives, and at crack of dawn, the servants in Hill House rise and prepare for their various arduous tasks. The small skivvy collects boots and starts polishing them. Cook lights the range and sets the kettles to boil. The under housemaid begins to get the fires laid, before carrying jugs of hot water up to the various rooms.

Meanwhile Marian takes the breakfast tray of cutlery up to the ground floor. But instead of laying the table, she slips into the master's study. It is a room she has not visited before. The air smells heavily of tobacco and hair oil. The wallpaper is dark red, the furniture dark wood and heavy in design.

There are several paintings of young women lying on sofas. They appear to be minimally clad, but she has no time to study them now. The crimson curtains are still drawn, adding to the shadowy atmosphere. Bluebeard's castle, she thinks, as she skims on light feet across the carpet to the master's desk. There is the box, its outer wrapping discarded and thrown carelessly into the waste-paper basket.

Cautiously, Marian lifts the lid and peers inside.

****

A few hours later, and oozing resentment from every pore, James William Malin Barrowclough presents himself at the front desk of Scotland Yard and asks for Detective Inspector Greig. He is shown into Greig's office at once. The two men face each other across Greig's desk. Although face-off might be a more appropriate term for the upcoming interview.

After a brief exchange of icy pleasantries, Greig fires the opening salvo. "I have now discovered the owner ~ or should I say, the former owner ~ of the top hat. I presume you know to which top hat I am referring?"

Barrowclough indicates sullenly that he does.

"The article in question belonged to your good self. It was handmade for you by Lock & Co. two years ago.

This is why I wrote to you. It appears that, despite your assertion that you did not recognise the dead man, there is a connection, albeit a tenuous one. Can you think of any reason why a hat belonging to you should be placed on the head of a dead man you claim you have no knowledge of ever meeting?"

Barrowclough folds his arms in a gesture that all detectives know to be a defensive pose. "This is your reason for summoning me from my place of business, is it, officer? A top hat. A hat that I clearly had no use for, and probably got one of my house servants to give to some old Jew to sell as second-hand goods? Does the word 'coincidence' not strike you as the obvious answer? In two years, I have probably got through several top hats. My servant disposes of them as they become unfit for my daily use. Have any of them appeared atop any corpses before?" he inquires, warming to his theme.

"Nevertheless," Greig persists, "I find the 'coincidence' as you call it … intriguing. There must be a reason for its reappearance in your garden. And for the decision by somebody to place the body of the man in such a specific location arranged in such an unusual way. Do you not see?"

Barrowclough bridles. "No, I do not see. I do not see at all. Let me repeat myself, officer: I did not know the unfortunate man. I did not contribute to his death. I do not know why he was left on my property. Or why he was wearing one of my top hats. And so, I request that you do not bother me or my family further. I have co-operated as far as I am able. I believe I mentioned that my wife has been unwell for some time. It is my duty to protect her and my boys from the unwelcome glare of any more adverse publicity. Do you understand? And now, if there is nothing else I can help you with, I have business to attend to, so I will bid you good day."

Barrowclough pushes himself to a stand. He does not offer his hand in farewell. Instead, he spins on his heel and stalks out of the office, his shoulders rigid with righteous indignation. Greig lets him depart. It is not what the man has said, but what he has not said, he thinks. The more Barrowclough tries to distance himself from events, the more Greig is sure there is a proximity. Or else why the reluctance to co-operate? The legal threats? The anger? It is indeed a tangled web. But he is determined to untangle it and reveal the truth that lies at the centre.

****

Meanwhile Marian, the new maidservant at Hill House, has a half-day. Precious time, to be spent in the company of her friend and fellow servant Dora, who also has a half-day. Dora is a personal ladies' maid, a position that Marian covets for herself. The two young women have agreed to meet at a local tearoom at three o'clock for tea, cakes and gossip, and so on the hour, wearing their finest bonnets, mantles and gloves, they enter the Lily Lounge Tearoom. They are shown to a nice table, close to the fire. They place their order.

"Well, Marian dear," Dora says, taking off her blue pigskin gloves and blowing into the fingers to straighten them. "How are you getting on at Hill House?"

The tall middle-aged woman dressed in black, who is busy clearing an adjacent table pauses, an empty teapot in her hand. She quietly sets it back down again and pretends to be very interested in the pattern on the check tablecloth.

"Oh, you know how it is, Dora," Marian replies. "Work, work, and more work. I shall be glad when the boys go back to Eton, though. Nasty pair. Think just coz they go to a fancy school they are better than the rest of us. Cheeky tykes. I've had to stop myself from giving the older one a right box on the ears many a time. If my mum had the bringing-up of him, he'd soon learn to mind his manners."

Dora laughs. "That's the good thing about Mrs Greville ~ no children. Just a visiting spinster niece, and she isn't any bother. As for the master, you hardly know he's in the house. She's got him well under her thumb."

"Oh, we ALL know when the master returns," Marian says tartly. She pauses, as a waitress starts unloading their tea-things. Once tea is poured, and cakes chosen and distributed, she beckons her companion to lean in. "There's something strange going on," she says. "First there was that dead man they found in the spinney. The one we're not meant to know anything about, of course. Now the master's started getting parcels. Small packages, wrapped in plain brown paper, same writing on each of the labels. Two so far. Every time one arrives, he whisks it away into his study and for the rest of the evening, my, is he in a foul mood. We walk on eggshells."

Dora's eyes light up. "Ooh, I LOVE a mystery. Go on, Marian, what's in the parcels?"

Marian cuts her piece of cake into small bite-size pieces before replying. "Now, that's the funny thing. I was dusting his study this morning, and he'd left one of the boxes on his desk, so of course I opened it up. And you'll never guess what was inside ..." she pauses, eying her companion slyly.

"Come on, don't leave me in suspense," her friend urges.

"Well then. It was a bird. A dead bird. A magpie. Now, isn't that uncanny?"

"One for sorrow," Dora says. "Isn't that what it means?"

"That's exactly what I thought. 'One for sorrow, two for joy' ~ the old nursery rhyme. Somebody sent my master a dead bird! Now, what do you make of that?"

Dora shakes her head. "I don't know what to make of it. It's certainly very strange. Where do the boxes come from, I wonder? Who sends them? And why? How thrilling! It's exactly like a story in a novel."

"That's what I thought too. Can't wait to see what happens next."

Lilith, standing motionless by the neighbouring table, holds her breath. Nor can she. As the talk passes on to the latest fashions and a certain footman who seems sweet on Dora, though his affections are not reciprocated, oh, indeed not, she quietly fills her tray with crockery and carries it back to the serving hatch. Then, leaving her able waitresses to run the tearoom for a while, she descends to the kitchen to write a quick letter.

As soon as the tearoom door closes this afternoon, she will pay a visit to her dear friend Josephine Greig, partly to pass on what she has just overheard, but also to see how she is faring in her pregnancy. She decides she will take a nice freshly baked cream sponge along with her rather startling information.

****

After sunset, when the lamplighter has run round the streets, and in the flickering yellow glow of the streetlamps, there is a moment when day stands on the threshold of night. The city seems to catch its breath. The workers have all left for hearth and home, and the people of the night are still preparing themselves for their nocturnal revelries.

Here, with their backs to a wall, wrapped in the same fur rug they rehomed from the stagecoach that carried them to London, the two runaways sit and watch the sky darken to velvet black above them and the pinprick stars come out. They have a bag of hot baked potatoes; they have a bottle of ginger beer. They sit in companionable silence, happy to be where they are, who they are.

The two have come a long way on their great adventure, but however far they have travelled, they cannot entirely shake off the place where they started out. The past casts a long shadow. Flitch and Liza's past casts an even longer one. While they sit and enjoy their supper and their new-found freedom, let us step back, albeit briefly, into that past.

****

It is an afternoon in late Summer, and they have been walking all day, the woman and the two small children. They carry their meagre possessions tied in blankets, everything they had time to pack before the bailiffs came to eject them from the cottage. The man of the family has left to find a better-paid job in another country, and the new landowner is eager to develop the land for housing, what with the railway passing so close on its way to Cambridge.

So, on they trudge, the woman and the two small children, silent, grim-faced. They had some bread earlier in the day, but that will be all they'll eat until they reach their destination, which is the great city of Cambridge. They enter the city at dusk and begin the thankless task of finding lodgings. But there are none to be had. Not for a woman with two children and no man. As night falls, the exhausted little family settles down under Victoria Bridge. They will stay here for two weeks. Every day, the woman will walk the streets, holes in her shoes, begging, looking for work, any work, anywhere and somewhere safe for her children to sleep.

Eventually, she will give up and the family, hungry and cold, will arrive at the iron gates leading to the Cambridge Union Workhouse in Mill Road to seek shelter. The Union, as it is known locally, is situated some distance from the town, to keep the poor away from the rich members of the university. It is the very last resort for the truly desperate.

After knocking on the door, they are let in, registered, and their belongings removed. Then comes the moment they have all been dreading. The woman tries to sweeten the parting. She tells the boy and his little sister that it is only for a short while ~ just until she gets back on her feet. She hugs them both, orders them to be good and obey the matron who will take care of them, and they will all be back together soon.

The woman goes to join the 'able-bodied women and girls over 16'. The girl is escorted to the 'girls between 7 and 16' room and the boy is taken to the 'youths and boys between 7 and 13'. Flitch and Liza will remain in the workhouse for three years. In all that time, they will never see their mother again.

****

Now, Flitch wipes his hand on his coat sleeve and sighs. "My eye, that was good." He looks down at his sister. "You enjoying yours?"

She nods, her small, pointed face still. "Flitch, I been meaning to ask ~ when he left, our Pa, where did he go?"

The boy makes a mouth. "Ma said he was going to take a ship to America, to find a good job and a nice place for us all to live. She said he'd write and send for us as soon as he could."

"He never did though, did he?"

The boy screws up his face. "He might of done, but where'd the letter go? Remember, the cottage was pulled down and we was put out on the street soon after he left us."

Silence falls as they think about that.

"Our Pa, do you think he ever came back to find us?"

The boy shrugs. "Dunno. But if'n he did, nobody'd knew where we went. Best not to think about it, Liza. We got food, somewhere to sleep, and we're doing alright."

"I guess so." The girl looks thoughtfully up at the night sky. "Funny to think the same stars are shining down on America. Maybe Pa's looking up at them right now and thinking about us. Like we are thinking about him."

The boy puts his arm round her shoulders and hugs her awkwardly. "We've got each other, Liza. Never forget that. And nobody is ever going to split us up again; I won't let them." He levers himself to his feet, holding out a hand to his sister. "Come on, let's go for a walk and look at all the shop windows before we turn in for the night. Busy day tomorrow."

She scrambles to her feet. "What's happening tomorrow, Flitch?" she asks.

He shrugs. "Don't know. But it will be busy. I promise," he grins. He tucks her arm under his and together they head towards the bright lights of the West End.

****

As Flitch and Liza set out to enjoy their free evening's entertainment in the seductive gas-lit streets, where all is dazzlement and delight, the scene changes to a small, derelict, backstreet public house known locally as the Cat & Cauliflower ~ nobody knows why, although over the years various unlikely explanations have been put forward.

Be that as it may, the Cat & Cauliflower lives up to its name in one respect: it always has a cat. No one knows where the cat comes from, but as one cat goes, it is presumed that somewhere, a call goes out: the Cat & Cauliflower has lost its cat, would the next incumbent please put in an appearance. The current cat is ginger and arrived in a rainstorm, its fur dripping on the sawdust floor, its furry face a picture of sadness and despair.

Here, in the back parlour, Sad Ginge is sitting on an unwiped bar, eyeing the plate of shrimps being consumed by Molly Marryat, a gaudily dressed 'soiled dove' who has just called in for 'a nip of something warming and a plate of something tasty'. Molly is one of the city's night workers, and she has been working Regent Street for some time, with nary a client.

Winter is hard on night workers like Molly. Whatever the weather, she has to display her charms and put in the requisite number of hours before dawn creeps over the windowsill. Failure to patrol her beat and display said charms to the passing male pedestrians means another girl, maybe younger, maybe more charming, maybe undercutting the going rate, could muscle in and take over her territory. It's a bit like the cat, but with less security of tenure.

As Molly enjoys her snack, watched intently by Sad Ginge, the public house door opens, admitting a swirl of cold foggy night air, and a man with a heavily-bearded Old Testament kind of face, wearing a dark shabby overcoat with its collar turned up, hat tipped forward over his brow. He is accompanied by another female night worker, who nods a friendly greeting to Molly as she leads her companion across the bar and up a flight of stairs at the back. The landlord of the Cat & Cauliflower rents out single rooms on an ad-hoc basis to ad-hoc individuals.

Molly observes their progress enviously while Sad Ginge seizes his chance, and hooks one of the shrimps. Ten minutes later, the man reappears. He orders a drink from the bar and gulps it down, before exiting at speed into the night. Molly waits. Sad Ginge waits.

Eventually Molly's co-worker re-enters the bar and joins her. "Giss us a glass of short, Harry," she says. She glances at Molly. "Need something to warm me up. That was a rum'un and no mistake." She sips the neat gin, wiping her mouth with her hand. "He had a funny accent, like he wasn't from round here. And he had this laugh ~ honest to God, Moll, it sounded like something you'd hear on a dark night in a graveyard. So I did the business and sent him on his way toot sweet, as they say." She tugs at her bonnet strings. "Right, you coming out, or what?"

Molly sighs. "Might as well."

The two leave the pub. Purring throatily, Sad Ginge creeps towards the unfinished plate of shrimps and starts eating. Meanwhile over in a quiet corner, Marcus Carrow, artist in a back booth and member of the Transformative Brotherhood, puts the finishing-touches to his evening's sketching, and quietly packs away his sketchbook. There are many morally outraged editors who will jump at the chance to publish realistic drawings of the sordid lives of those who make a living from the streets, even more so when their clients are also included. Plus, he needs the drawings he's done for a triptych called Morning, Noon and Night, a work he intended to show in the Transformative Brotherhood's upcoming exhibition.

****

Morning arrives and a pale-yellow sun is fighting a losing battle with the smoke from a million chimneys as

James William Malin Barrowclough alights from a cab and makes his way to the office building close to Paddington railway station, where Barrowclough and Cuthbert, Land Agents, have their headquarters. He greets the building's porter and is handed a copy of his daily newspaper of choice, which has been carefully ironed, prior to his arrival, in the porter's tiny back room.

Barrowclough checks the headlines, finds to his satisfaction that he is no longer front-page news, and climbs the stairs to the first floor, where two female typewriters are already busily tapping and pinging their way through their morning tasks. It always unsettles him to see these women working, but as Richard Cuthbert has pointed out on many occasions, women are cheaper to employ than men, and far more expendable as there is an endless supply of them all eagerly waiting to enter the workforce.

Nevertheless, Barrowclough nervously edges past the female staff, merely uttering a perfunctory greeting, and scuttles into his office, closing the door. The morning post has been placed on his desk, along with a couple of official legal documents that require his signature. He glances through them ~ speculative land purchases agreed with a variety of freeholders close to the proposed route of a new railway. The land is eminently suitable for building upon.

Barrowclough signs his name with a flourish. Once his partner has appended his signature, they will arrange for the land to be divided into various plots, maybe getting some of their own building contractors to construct a few show houses to show what might be achieved. Then they will offer the rest of the plots to be 'let out on building leases'.

As soon as the land has been apportioned off (ground rent fixed at 5 guineas a year) and the speculative builders have thrown up a number of houses,

Barrowclough & Cuthbert will sell the ground rents at auction, as ground rents are considered to be the safest investments, for if not paid, Barrowclough and Cuthbert, as the original landowners, have the right to seize the houses.

This is how they have both prospered; how they have enriched themselves. In Barrowclough's case, his riches have also given him access to a social class he could never have entered: the sort of people who have good birth but little fortune, resulting in a large house in Hampstead, a wife who is considerably above him in social status and a set of servants who are considerably below, but still regard him as inferior, such are the mores of London servants. He also has entrée to various clubs, and now two sons at a top public school. But life has a habit of bowling googlies, as he is just about to discover.

Having signed the land acquisitions, Barrowclough shouts for one of the typewriters to attend him. A second's pause, and the door opens. "I brought you your mid-morning coffee, sir," says the young woman. He does not remember her name. "And this package has just been delivered, sir. Shall I put it on your desk with the coffee?"

He nods, not looking up. The young woman carefully sets down a bone china cup full of a milky brew, two biscuits in the saucer, and a small brown-paper wrapped package. She makes a small forward motion with her upper body, which could be interpreted as a formal bow, not that he notices, and leaves the office. Alone, Barrowclough sits on, his eyes fixed on the package, a sense of chill apprehension creeping over him as his coffee cools.

A few hours later, Barrowclough leaves his office and heads to a backstreet hostelry for a hot lunch, which he washes down with a large brandy. He has chosen it as he is pretty sure none of those who know him in his 'other' professional role favour it with their custom. Sometimes even rats have the urge to get out of the race for a while. The place is full of city clerks refreshing themselves on cheap cuts of meat, floury potatoes and watery beer.

By the time he returns to his office, Barrowclough, fortified by alcohol and bravado, has shaken off his earlier dread. He summons a typewriter, hands her the unopened package and tells her to get rid of it at once. Then he applies himself to the correspondence and documents that have arrived over the morning period.

Tea is brought mid-afternoon in the same cup, along with a letter from a certain developer. He made an offer for some of the land Barrowclough and Cuthbert had acquired in anticipation of the beginnings of the excavations for a circular underground line. Now, he requests a meeting with either partner to discuss the progress of the offer. The offices are in Farringdon Street. The letter is dated today.

In the absence of Cuthbert, who is out of town pursuing further land acquisitions, Barrowclough decides to take the initiative and call round. The offer is not nearly high enough, and in such cases, it is always prudent to negotiate the price upwards personally. He writes a quick reply, which he dispatches with one of the small messenger boys who serve the four companies in the building.

Barrowclough leaves the building. A cold rain is falling steadily out of a leaden sky. He hails a cab, and a short while later arrives at the offices of the developer. The ensuing meeting runs to the accustomed script. The developer is disabused of the validity of his offer and given a deadline to improve it. Barrowclough leaves. The rain has not let up and there are no cabs to be seen. He decides to take the underground train back to his office. After a short walk and a stepped descent, he finds himself standing on the wooden platform, peering into the long dark tunnel. The underground railway is a marvel of modern engineering. If only Barrowclough and Cuthbert had been around to buy up the residential land right at the start, they would be millionaires by now, he thinks.

Barrowclough sees the lights of the arriving train approaching like the two eyes of some ferocious monster. At the same time, he becomes aware of somebody standing close behind him. Very close. He can feel warm breath on the back of his neck. Admittedly, the platform is busy, but he sees no reason for anybody to be in such close proximity. He is just about to turn round and issue a rebuke when the train rushes into the station. As it shrieks its arrival, someone places their hands flat on Barrowclough's back and gives him a sharp shove. Mouth opening in shock, he falls through the air, landing heavily across the rails directly in the path of the oncoming train. There is a shout, a screech of brakes, followed by a shocked silence.

Then a hubbub breaks out on the platform. A couple of men try to get under the train to reach the victim. Women begin to cry or scream hysterically. Others surge forward to take a look. Passengers inside the carriages, who do not realise what has happened, start beating on the windows and doors, demanding to be let out.

Eventually, the platform guard and station manager restore order. At their command, a corridor is created to allow passengers to alight. Those who did not witness the accident are also ordered to leave the station at the same time. The train is driven slowly backwards until the body is revealed. A medical team from the nearby hospital arrives with a stretcher. A couple of constables also turn up and begin to take names, addresses and statements from those who claim to have stood close to the unfortunate man, and seen what happened. Or thought they saw what happened. Meanwhile, above ground, as the news of the accident spreads, the usual crowd assembles to share, process and mythologise the event. In time, some journalists join them, notebooks and pencils ready.

The evening newspapers will carry the story: **'Tragic Accident! Man Falls to his death at Farringdon Station! Is the London underground railway really safe? Expert warnings ignored!'** This will be followed by a couple of days of lurid stories of almost every kind of subterranean near fatality that the inventive London public can come up with.

The only story missing from the dramatic spewings of the newspapers and the notebooks of the police officers will be that of the bearded man in the dark shabby overcoat who slipped quietly through the panicking platform crowd and made his way back to the surface.

****

The following morning finds Detective Inspector Greig giving the benefit of his years of experience to his junior colleague Detective Constable Tom Williams as the two pore over the coroner's report on the body found in the grounds of Hill House.

"As you can see, Tom, the coroner does not find any evidence of human interference in the death," Greig says. "There are no stab wounds, no traces of poison, no bruising ~ nothing to infer that this unfortunate man met his end in any other way than by natural circumstances."

"Is starving to death on the city streets a 'natural circumstance', Mr. Greig?" Williams inquires.

"Sadly, in a great city like London, it happens far more than either you or I would care to contemplate,"

Greig says. "As does suicide of the elderly. You've seen the reports from the river police? So many older people prefer to throw themselves into the river rather than face a long cold hungry winter, or the shame of going to the workhouse."

The young officer pulls a face. Greig continues quickly: "That's why the Metropolitan Police needs good men like you, Tom. Men who have a conscience and are prepared to put their opinions into practice. But in this case, we have reached a dead end." He winces at the unfortunate choice of words. "There is nothing other than circumstantial evidence to link Mr. Barrowclough with the death of the vagrant. And the gentleman has made it quite clear, in no uncertain terms, that he is not prepared to speak to us further on the matter or cooperate with us in tracking down the perpetrator. And as nobody has come forward to claim the man, we shall have to consign him to a pauper's grave. Yes, I am as sorry as you are. Now then, how are you getting on with that legal manual I gave you to study?"

"I'm making progress, Mr. Greig. I shall not let you down when I sit my exams."

"I am sure you will not, Tom. I have every confidence in your abilities. As does Detective Inspector Stride. One day soon you will make a very fine officer." Greig signs the coroner's report and hands it over to Williams to take down to the basement.

As the two men walk across the front foyer of Scotland Yard, Greig hears his name being called. He glances round. A man is sitting on the Anxious Bench. He recognises him immediately. It is the surly servant from Hill House, but this time his face has a very worried expression. He rises and approaches the two detectives.

"Sir, I was hoping you'd be here. My master has not been home since yesterday morning. His bed was not slept in last night and we have had no word from him since he left for work after breakfast that day."

Greig notes the 'sir'. "Is this unusual?"

"Oh yes, sir. Extremely. The master always tells me or sends word if he is going to be home late, in case something happens to Mrs Barrowclough or one of the boys and I need to get hold of him in a hurry. What do you think has happened?"

Greig shakes his head. "Impossible to say. Maybe someone in his office might know? Have you asked?"

The servant shakes his head. "I came straight here, sir. Thinking it was the best thing to do ~ after that other business."

Greig steers him back to the bench. "I see. Well, I suggest you go and make a list of all the places he might have visited, and any close friends he might be staying with. Then call round and see what you can find out. I have to say that most people who 'disappear' unexpectedly usually turn up in a few days, generally with a perfectly logical explanation for their absence. I suggest you ask at his place of work first. They may know where he was going yesterday."

"Yes, sir. I will do that. And what will you do in the meantime, sir?" the servant asks.

"I shall wait," Greig says. "And I will keep my eyes and ears open. There is nothing here to alarm yourself or the Barrowclough family at present. There could be a very simple reason: your master was taken unwell overnight or perhaps overindulged at table and decided to stay at an hotel. If he fails to come home in the next few days, we will start to make our own inquiries." He smiles in what he hopes is a reassuring manner.

"If you say so, sir," the servant rises, reluctantly. Greig walks him to the door. "Please let me know if we can be of any further assistance," he says politely, ushering him out into the street. Once the manservant has left, Greig turns to his young companion. "Well Tom, what is your assessment?"

"It's puzzling, Mr. Greig. Mr. Barrowclough says he didn't know the dead man. The coroner didn't find any signs the man was murdered. There is the link of the top hat ~ but as we know, clothes get sold on and are worn by other people," he pauses. "And now ..."

And now, Greig thinks. And now? He recalls what Lilith told him about the mysterious parcel, the dead bird. The way the man was so hostile and reluctant to cooperate. Is Barrowclough being blackmailed by somebody? Has he temporarily gone to ground somewhere? Whatever the case, until something further emerges, there is nothing to be done. London is a huge city. He could be anywhere. They do not have the manpower to cover every corner of it.

"Do you still want me to file these notes?" Williams asks, indicating the folder under his arm.

Greig considers this. Hesitates. Then reaches a decision. "Perhaps not. Let's leave it out for now, Tom. After all, what's a few more days? We have nothing to lose, have we?"

****

Meanwhile, Richard Cuthbert, land speculator and partner of the currently missing Barrowclough, is returning to his Paddington office after a successful trip to the North. The further the railway extends its tentacles, the more opportunities lie waiting for a good land speculator with a nose for prospective opportunities and few scruples.

He has managed to secure land and properties along what will soon, according to his spies, be a section of the secondary route up the west coast of Scotland. He has also transferred all the rents of the properties to the company, and appointed rent collectors to apprise the occupants of the steep rent rise that they must now swallow under their new landlord.

A good job, well done. In time, if his speculations prove correct, his team of rent collectors will swiftly morph into evictors, and the families will be put out onto the street, to go wherever the four winds take them, and shift for themselves. They are not his concern. The cleared land will then be offered to the private railway company at a competitive rate ~ in that it is either purchase at his price or re-route the entire line completely.

Cuthbert is looking forward to sharing his success with his business partner, and thus his step is light and his air jaunty as he enters the outer office and greets 'the girls' as he privately refers to the female staff, who glance up briefly from their machines as he marches towards Barrowclough's office.

"He isn't in yet, Mr. Cuthbert," one of the young women informs him.

Cuthbert's eyebrows rise. "Really? That is unusual. Hmm. Perhaps he is unwell or has an early meeting. Let me check his desk diary."

He enters his partner's office and advances to the desk. Everything looks neat and tidy. Pens in the tray, blotter unused and a pile of documents stacked neatly to one side. He opens Barrowclough's diary. It has nothing entered for the previous day. No meetings, no lunch appointments. As he stands there, trying to puzzle out what might have happened, one of the young women enters the room. She is carrying a small box.

"Excuse me, sir. This was delivered yesterday. Mr. Barrowclough seemed a bit upset about it. I was supposed to get rid of it, but we had a lot of work to do, and I forgot. I am sorry, sir."

Cuthbert takes the box from her. "Never mind. Thank you, Miss Voss. You may go." He sets the box down on the desk and regards it thoughtfully. There are times in their business relationship when Richard Cuthbert suspects he is not being told everything he needs to know about his partner's dealings. Barrowclough frequently maintains a level of secrecy that is, frankly, rather annoying.

Perhaps this is another of those things that he isn't being told about, but ought to be? There is only one way to find out. After all, the package was sent to their joint office, and it is not marked 'private', so surely he has every right to see what it contains. He picks up the box and rips off the brown paper covering. A few minutes later, Richard Cuthbert barrels out of his office, informs the typewriters brusquely that he is stepping out, and is not sure exactly when he will return.

****

Meanwhile, a train pulls into Cambridge station and huffs to a halt by the buffers. A man steps out of a second-class railway carriage and walks along the platform. He surrenders his ticket at the barrier and, after making a few judicious inquiries, leaves the station at a brisk pace.

Having traversed the densely populated streets that surround the railway station and asked directions of several passers-by, the man eventually arrives on the doorstep of the Union Workhouse. He pulls the bell rope. For a while, nothing happens. He waits on the step. Finally, the door is opened by a small, wizened child in a sack-coloured frock, a pair of men's boots and an oversized apron. There is a bucket of water at her feet, and she holds a dripping cloth in one hand. She stares up at him.

"We're not open," she informs him.

The man looks down at her, pity in his eyes. He wears a warm woollen overcoat, a bright yellow muffler and a brown tweed cap. He moves his gaze and stares over her shoulder, taking in bare whitewashed walls, devoid of any ornament except for a portrait of the Queen. He sees a threadbare carpet barely reaching to the skirting board. His nostrils pick up the sour odour of bodies, drains and over-cooked food of a cabbage, bad meat and gruel nature.

"I haven't come to seek admittance," he tells the child. "I want to find out if my wife and children are here."

There is the sound of heavy footsteps, and a man appears behind the child. He is rotund, bald but with a frill of red hair around the lower part of his skull. His eyes are small and piercing-blue and his small nose is turned up. He wears an apron over a loud check suit. The impression is of a clothed pig walking on its hind legs. The pig eyes the caller slowly from head to foot, then folds its arms in a hostile fashion.

"Run along, child. I'll deal with this. And take that bucket with you."

The small girl hesitates, her face set in a mulish expression of obstinacy. "I ain't a child. My name is Bella. An' I was told by Mrs Farish to clean the front step and mind the door. Which is what I was doing."

The pig, who is in reality the overseer of the workhouse, waves her away, then turns his attention to the visitor. "Yes? You are inquiring about some of our residents, is that correct?"

The man indicates that is his mission and to do so, he wishes to enter the workhouse. He speaks with an American accent which means, in the overseer's eyes, that he is a foreigner, so must be treated with great suspicion. Reluctantly, the overseer steps aside and allows him to enter. He walks ahead of the man, stopping at a closed door.

"We can talk in here," he says, producing a ring of keys and unlocking the door. The man follows him into the room. There is a desk but there are no chairs, so both men stand, one behind, one in front of the desk. On the desk is a big ledger and a pen and inkstand. The overseer opens the ledger.

"If you can give me the date when you think they came here, I can see whether they are still with us."

The man shakes his head. "Can't be done. I've been out of the country for some time. I came back, meaning to find them. But when I got to our village, I found my cottage had been knocked down to make way for a railway yard. Some people in the village told me my wife and children had been turned out on the street and had gone to Cambridge to find shelter and work. I've been walking the streets ever since, asking and searching, day and night. It was pure luck I met a woman who recollected seeing them entering this place. I can give you their names. Will that do?"

The overseer scratches his bald pate. "It's h'irregular. Everything needs to be done by the book. This book, see. There are rules and laws and regulations, and they have to be followed at all times."

The man rolls his eyes. "Look, my name is Sam Thomas. My wife's name is Elizabeth Thomas. My son is Frederick Thomas ~ we call him Flitch ~ and my girl is Eliza Thomas." He draws himself up to his full height and glares at the overseer. "Now, I'm going to ask you once again: are they here? And you better answer me, coz I'm handy with my fists, and I ain't afraid to knock you down. I know what these places are like and if they are here, I'm taking them away with me. Now then. What've you got to say?"

The overseer closes the book and pulls a face. "No need for that language. I will go and make inquiries. You wait here."

He goes out, closing the door. The man waits. He walks about the room, stares out of a small window that looks onto a bleak, deserted yard. Time passes. Then the door is quietly opened, and the small, wizened girl reappears. "You Liza's Pa?" she asks in a whispered voice. "I heard what you said."

The man nods. The girl edges into the room. He notices how red and chapped her hands are; her thin wrists poke out of her ragged sleeves. "I shared a bed with Liza."

The man focuses in on her face. "You say 'you shared'; does that mean she is no longer here?"

The child shakes her head. "She ran away. With her brother. She climbed out the window in the night. There's a bit where the bars is loose."

The man stares at her incredulously. "You're sure that's what happened? When?"

She nods. "I'm sure as sure, mister. It was after Christmastime. I remember we went to the police station for new boots. Me and Liza's boots were too tight. That was when she said she and her brother were going to run away. It was a secret. I nivver told. She said nivver to tell a soul, and I din't. Even when they beat me coz I shared her bed, so they said I must've known. Only telling you now, coz you're her Pa. She and Flitch, they were going to get as far away from here as they could."

His eyes never leave her face. "Did she tell you where they were going?"

She bites her lower lip. "I FINK she might of said they was going to strike out for London." She gives him a crooked smile. "I hope you find them. If you do, tell her Bella nivver told. Coz I didn't." And with that, she is gone, leaving the man to frown and shake his head in bewilderment at the unexpected turn of events.

He waits on. Eventually, the overseer returns. He does not make eye contact. "Well, I have to tell you, sir, that your family isn't here anymore. No."

"Where has my wife gone?" the man asks.

"She took ill, back of last year. A low fever. It was bad. I'm sorry. A lot of the women had it." He does not offer any further elaboration, leaving the man to draw the obvious conclusion.

"Where is she buried?"

The overseer has the grace to look slightly ashamed. "She was buried on the parish. I can tell you where she lies, if you wish to visit the ground."

"A pauper's burial?" The man's face is tight, his breath comes fast.

The overseer fiddles with the ledger. He looks off. "She had the best medical treatment, I'm sure," he says. It is a statement so clearly untrue that the man does not dignify it with a response.

"And my two children?" He knows the response, but he wants to hear it from this man's lips. Wants him to feel shame.

"They ain't here no more neither. They run away ~ yes, after everything what we did for them. Nursing their mother, burying her, and that's how they repaid us. Ungrateful pair."

The man makes no reply to this accusation. The silence that descends is as cold and desolate as the room itself. Eventually, the man reaches into his inner coat pocket. "This is my business card. If you hear anything about my children ~ anything at all, please send me a telegram."

The overseer grabs the card and stuffs it into his apron pocket. Then there is nothing more to say. He directs the man to the parish burial ground. The door to the Union

Workhouse closes behind him. The iron gate closes behind him. It is as if the past is closing behind him too. The past in which there was a cottage, a home, a family.

The man turns his back on the place and makes his way to the parish graveyard, where there are no headstones, just rank weeds and a few straggly bushes. Life passed so quickly; you could scarcely believe it. One minute you were in its embrace. The next minute, it let you go.

He removes his hat and leans on the wooden fence, staring at the untended ground. There are many freshly dug mounds of bare earth. His wife could be lying under any of them. Bitter thoughts tear at him like claws. He should never have left England. He should have written more letters. If only he'd returned sooner. Time slides past. The wind blows dead leaves at his feet. A few crows circle above his head. Eventually, he replaces his cap and turns his face towards Cambridge. Tonight, he will stay at an hotel. Tomorrow, he will catch the first morning train to London. There is a brief window of opportunity to search for his lost children before his ship leaves for New York.

****

As Sam Thomas, Flitch and Liza's father, makes his way to Cambridge to find somewhere to dine and spend the night, back in London, Detective Inspector Greig is about to receive an unexpected visitor in the form of Inspector Lambert Elliot of Paddington Police Office. The visitor is accompanied by a business-suited individual, whom he introduces to the desk duty officer as Mr. Richard Cuthbert of Barrowclough & Cuthbert.

Lachlan Greig greets the Inspector politely ~ they have cooperated recently on the successful investigation into a multiple murder, but his eyebrows rise in surprise when the business name of his companion is introduced. He immediately wipes his features of all expression, shows both men into his small office, and waits to hear why they are here.

Richard Cuthbert is a big fidgety man. He sits awkwardly on the small hard chair, fusses with the creases in his trousers, then pulls at the ends of his moustache. He clears his throat. Greig waits. In his experience, sometimes you understand more in someone's silence than in their words. People can hide behind words. What this man's silence is saying is: I am afraid of something I do not understand.

After the silence has hung around for a bit longer, Cuthbert clears his throat, and hands Greig a piece of paper. "One of my office girls gave me this today. I have been away from my office for a week. On my return, I was told that my partner, Mr. James Barrowclough, had received a small parcel yesterday, which seemed to have upset him. He left the office shortly afterwards and has not been seen in the office since.

"I was given the parcel and took the liberty of opening it." He swallows. "Inside, inspector, was the skull of a dead bird. Rotting. There were maggots crawling in and out of the eye sockets. I couldn't believe what I saw. And the smell ~ quite disgusting. And underneath the wrapping was a piece of paper, folded small."

He hands the paper to Greig, who unfolds it and studies it intently. The message is brief and written in a strangely cramped hand, as if by a child. The letters hop and jump around. *"Seven for a secret."* Somehow, Greig feels no surprise. It is as if this piece of the mystery that began with a dead man covered in snow has been waiting, just beyond the horizon. And now it is here.

"Of course, I took the box straight to the local police. But what does the message mean, inspector?" Cuthbert bleats, wringing his hands. "Why send it to our office along with a dead bird's skull? And what has become of my business partner?"

"These are indeed very serious questions," Greig says, pursing his mouth. "And I am afraid I do not have the answers, Mr. Cuthbert. Not right at this moment. But I shall do, I assure you. And when I have them, you will be informed. Now, if you would care to leave the paper with me ~ I am grateful to you and to my colleague for alerting me to its presence. I suggest you return to your office; perhaps Mr. Barrowclough may have turned up in your absence? Let us hope so. Trust me, you will be kept abreast of any developments this end."

Greig rises from his seat, indicating by the gesture that the meeting is over. He shows the two men out, then returns to his desk, spreading the paper out in front of him. A man who takes the time to compose a strangely menacing message. An individual so focused on revenge that he plants a dead body on the land of his victim, destroys birds and sends their corpses through the postal service. What lies behind his actions? Is it revenge? If so, for what? What offence has the rather unpleasant uncooperative Mr. Barrowclough perpetrated? And where on earth is he now?

At the end of the day, having heard nothing from Barrowclough's servant, nor from Richard Cuthbert ~ which could mean anything or nothing, Greig makes his way back to the house in St Johns Wood where his beloved wife and his supper are waiting. It has been a frustrating day.

He finds his wife Josephine going through a large ledger, in the company of her faithful business manager Trafalgar Moggs, who previously served her uncle as clerk of King & Co., the business Josephine has inherited. They have their heads bent over a page. Pencils are being used as gesturing tools and an empty coffee pot shows that some serious work has been taking place. Greig sighs. He wishes his wife would put her feet up and rest but knows better than to utter his thoughts aloud in her presence.

Josephine rises from her chair as he enters the room. She supports her back with her two palms. "Supper is nearly ready," she says, smiling and reaching up to plant a kiss on his cheek. "Mr. Moggs and I have just finished last month's figures."

"Is everything going well?" Greig asks, because he has learned that showing an interest in his wife's business makes for a better relationship.

"We are maintaining steady progress," she replies brightly, because she has learned that supplying a general response indicates that she appreciates his attempts at showing an interest in her business.

Greig nods. Then, addressing them both, "What do you know about magpies?" he inquires.

They both regard him in a startled fashion. It is not the sort of question one expects. Moggs scratches his chin. "They're thieving creatures. They steal things," he says. "Gold, silver, anything shiny."

Josephine agrees. "Isn't there a rhyme about them: One for sorrow, two for joy … something like that?"

Moggs takes up the narrative. "I remember that rhyme from my childhood: Three for a girl, four for a boy. Five for silver, six for gold. Seven for a secret, never to be told, and I remember too that my mother hated them. She always used to cross herself whenever she saw one. 'Devil, I defy thee' she'd say. Nonsense of course. They're just birds after all."

Greig stares at him. "Did she say that indeed," he murmurs.

"Is there anything else I can tell you, Mr. Greig?" Moggs asks.

Greig shakes his head. "Most helpful," he says thoughtfully. "Thank you, Mr. Moggs."

"Then if you will excuse me, I shall leave you now, Miss King," says Trafalgar Moggs who is a man of habit, which currently dictates that his boss retains the company name regardless of relinquishing her single status. "I bid you both a pleasant evening." He bows and is shown out into the hall by the servant.

"Magpies?" Josephine queries when they are alone.

He shrugs. "A query that came up at work."

The servant returns to announce that dinner is ready.

Greig and his wife move to the dining room. Soup is served. Greig stirs his soup round and round his bowl, staring down into its murky depths as if seeking a solution to what is currently on his mind. After a few minutes, Josephine sets down her own spoon and observes him across the table.

"Is the soup not to your liking, Lachlan? I thought a nice bowl of Scotch broth would warm you up on this cold day."

Greig puts down his spoon. "It is delicious, thank you. But I have a lot upon my mind at the moment. A troubling case that is currently defying my best thinking." He smiles at her. "But I am sure things will become clearer after this good dinner. See, I am eating it now."

Josephine shakes her head at him. She has been through this so many times since they married. Her husband's way of dealing with an investigation is to absorb himself completely in its complexities. She suspects the magpies may have something to do with his present preoccupation.

Previously, she might have discussed it with him, helped him to tease out the strands of whatever it was that perplexed him. Now, she has other concerns. The child lies heavily within her, and although she has been reassured by various female acquaintances that giving birth is something all married women go through and emerge safely the other side, she cannot help feeling apprehensive at the prospect, which each day brings ever closer.

A grilled sole, mutton stew and some bottled plums are consumed in relative silence. Then Greig excuses himself and retires to his study to think things out. Alas, by the time candles are brought, he has still got no further in his cogitations, other than to decide he will have to await further developments. Unbeknown to him, the first of them is even now being delivered in vans to various newsagents.

****

'There is no more striking sight in London than the bustle of its great streets,' so writes John Murray in his *Handbook of Modern London.* And here, handbook in hand, are Monsieur and Madame Avignon, accompanied by their manservant Plouc. They are studying the famous Clue Map, depicting the main thoroughfares, landmarks and railway lines, followed by the city's *'main divisions and characteristic features' (ibid).*

It is their fourth day in the capital and, thus far, it compares most unfavourably with their home city of Paris. The streets are dirty, there are no wide, tree-lined boulevards along which to stroll, the people push and shove and swear, and as for the food! Execrable barely covers it. The bread tastes of nothing, the wine is sour. They suspect that their delicate and refined French digestions are not suited to the English diet. Yesterday evening, they unwisely ordered something called a meat pie. They are still suffering from the aftereffects.

Monsieur Avignon, an exporter of fine furniture in the Louis XIV style (elaborate scrolly bits and gold

78

paint), has a meeting with a prospective department store buyer later this morning to set up an import account, after which the trio intend to visit Madame Tussaud's waxwork exhibition. But right now, the three enter a small coffee house, where three cups of something they all suspect will be undrinkable are requested. While they wait, Monsieur Avignon orders Plouc to fetch a copy of a daily newspaper, to pass the time.

The newspaper is brought and spread out on the table. They sit and contemplate the front page. Then Plouc gives an exclamation of surprise. He points to a headline and to the picture of a top-hatted man, falling in a graceful arc onto the rails as a train speeds towards him.

"Ce monsieur ~ moi, je l'ai vu!" he cries.

Further close questioning by his employers reveals that Plouc had caught the underground railway, having desired to take a trip during the couple of hours he had free. While waiting for the train to arrive, he found himself standing next to the gentleman in the picture. The story is read aloud by Monsieur Avignon in rough translation. Plouc shakes his head. That was not what happened, he says. In his version, he distinctly saw another man reach out and deliberately push the victim in front of the train. His account is regarded with scepticism by Monsieur, disbelief by Madame, nevertheless Plouc sticks stubbornly to his tale.

The undrinkable coffee is brought, and during its consumption, it is decided that Plouc's evidence needs to be presented to someone in authority. If the man's untimely death was not suicide, but occurred at the hands of another, this should be revealed, and the culprit identified and brought to justice. It is the French way. There is little time to spare, and thus Plouc (who speaks limited English) and Madame Avignon (who is reasonably fluent) are put into a hansom, with the driver being told to take them to Scotland Yard *'tout de suite'*.

There is a difference between intention and outcome ~ in this case it is the volume of traffic, and so it takes some time before the hansom pulls up outside Scotland Yard and disgorges its two foreign passengers. Plouc and Madame mount the steps, and after a lot of hand-waving, broken English and misunderstanding on all sides, are shown by the day constable to the Anxious Bench to await the arrival of one of the detectives, who unfortunately for the visitors turns out to be Detective Inspector Stride, as Greig and young Williams have been unexpectedly called away on another case.

Stride's attitude towards the many foreigners who inhabit the city could best be described as 'problematic', and at worst as 'bordering on intolerant' so the omens are not good as the two French citizens follow him to his dust-laden, untidy office, where Madame carefully wipes down the chair she is offered with a lace handkerchief before lowering herself cautiously onto it.

Luckily for all parties concerned, Detective Constable Williams, who has a smattering of French and a better attitude, will arrive back at Scotland Yard shortly and be directed to Stride's office. The ensuing interview will then free itself from the rocks of mutual antipathy and set sail into the smoother waters of important communication.

Inspector Greig returns just as Plouc is taken by Williams to meet the police artist, who will attempt to create a likeness of the man with the heavy beard, dark eyes, and shabby black overcoat, who slipped away into the crowd, even as his victim was falling to his death under the wheels of the train.

"Mr. Stride called them 'you Frenchies' to their faces, Mr. Greig," Williams says sadly, after leaving the servant with Leonard, the artist. "Luckily, I'm not sure they understood."

Greig eye rolls in sympathy. He has had to bite his tongue many a time when the subject of one of the many foreign communities comes up. Mind, Stride is just as vituperative about politicians, civil servants, and members of the fourth estate, and in this, he heartily agrees with him.

"I might be speaking out of turn, Mr. Greig," Williams continues, "but I was thinking of Mr. Barrowclough. We know he hasn't been seen for a while. We know he was sent a threatening package with a warning and now, it seems a man was deliberately pushed under a train. What do you think, sir? Am I barking up the wrong tree? Because I'm getting a strong suspicion, especially after what the young French gentleman said, that the man pushed under the train was Mr. Barrowclough himself. So maybe the man who pushed him was the one who sent the packages to his house and office? Possibly the same man who left the body in his garden."

"That's called a hunch, Tom," Greig says, nodding. "And it's how detection works. Always follow your suspicions, however implausible they may appear at first; nine times out of ten, they will be correct. In this case, I think it's the right tree and the right dog as well. Now, I'll tell you what we're going to do: we'll send a message round to various police offices in the area to ascertain where the body of the railway accident victim is being held, as it is possibly the subject of a murder inquiry."

Williams agrees, relieved that his suggestion hasn't been dismissed out of hand. "Leave it with me; I'll deal with it at once, Mr. Greig," he says and hurries away.

The response to the plea for information comes back swiftly: the body has been transferred to the morgue at

University College Hospital. Greig immediately writes to the hospital, requesting that Scotland Yard detectives might visit the morgue to take a look at the body before any coroner's inquest is arranged, as new evidence has just emerged concerning the cause of the man's death.

And so, later that afternoon and accompanied by Detective Constable Tom Williams, Greig hastens to University College Hospital and is shown into the morgue by one of the porters, where the mangled body of Mr. James William Malin Barrowclough lies upon a metal gurney, awaiting identification.

****

The funeral of James William Malin Barrowclough takes place on a chilly, sunless day. There might be snowdrops and crocuses in the ornamental garden at the back of Hill House, but there is straw on the gravel at the front, and black bows decorate the pillars on either side of the door. All the windows have their blinds drawn and the house seems to have withdrawn into itself. By eleven, the glass-sided hearse, drawn by four black-plumed horses, is waiting outside, followed by a procession of carriages with their blinds also drawn down out of respect.

Beyond the gate, a large crowd has gathered to witness the final journey of the local businessman whose untimely death has featured in the local newspaper in lurid and unlikely detail, as well as further afield. Interest has also doubled as the link between the dead body encased in snow and the dead man killed by the underground train has been revealed. Nothing like two terrible tragedies occurring within a short space of time to the same family to draw a ghoulish crowd.

There is, however, much sympathy for the invalid widow and the two boys, now left alone and fatherless.

Much anger is directed towards the Metropolitan Underground Railway, which is seen as the source of far too many mishaps. Stories of near misses on platforms, falling down steps and the careless attitude of staff in general are swapped and shared to the mutual satisfaction of the assembled multitude.

In time, the front door of Hill House opens, and a hush falls on the crowd as the oak coffin, its brass handles gleaming, and draped in a simple black velvet cloth, is carried down the steps by the pallbearers. It is followed by the family, also clad in black. Particular attention is paid to the Barrowclough widow, whose presence in the matrimonial home has been the subject of much speculation over the years, the rumours being that she died in childbirth/of a wasting disease/or was mad/had been locked in an attic/and was being starved to death by her cruel husband.

Nobody has the slightest recollection of ever seeing her and sadly, they are not getting much of a sight of her now, given her full black veil, close bonnet, gloves and voluminous black gown and mantle. She is helped up the steps of the first carriage and disappears from view, along with her youngest son.

The older boy positions himself at the rear of the hearse, just ahead of the senior household servants as the horses are turned, and the coffin passes through the gates. Hats are whipped off heads as a mark of respect and the hearse progresses slowly down the hill to the church, passing, on its journey, a bearded man in a shabby dark overcoat, his hat pulled well down over his face, who is watching the funeral procession from the shelter of a convenient doorway.

As soon as the last carriage has clopped its way along the cobbled street, the man steps out and attaches himself to the back of the crowd. Assuming the air of a casual onlooker, he strides amongst them until the hearse halts outside the small proprietary chapel in Downshire Hill. The man then threads his way through the throng, and enters the chapel, making his way up the stairs to the gallery where he sits at the back. Alone.

The service is conducted by a minister who clearly has had little contact with the deceased during his lifetime. Words of a laudatory nature are uttered. Statements of assumed piety are made. The eternal destination of Barrowclough's soul is asserted. The immediate family, seated in the front of the boxed pews bow their heads. A few handkerchiefs are produced by the congregation. Up in the gallery, the man's face is expressionless.

Finally, the service grinds to its end. The man slips out during the final hymn. From the waiting crowd, he ascertains that the body of the deceased will be taken to the fashionable necropolis of Highgate cemetery, where it will be buried in style, with a fancy headstone, as befits a man of status and wealth.

He walks away. Reaching the High Street, he enters a public house, where he installs himself in a back booth and orders a glass of ale and a steak pie and peas. As he waits for his food to arrive, the man helps himself to a copy of the local paper. He shows particular interest in the list of local deaths and funeral arrangements. His meal arrives and is consumed in silence. After finishing it, he takes the knife and furtively cuts out the list of deaths, placing it in his pocket. He sits on as the afternoon slips away and darkness settles around the corners of his mind and creeps slowly inwards.

****

Highgate Cemetery consists of thirty-nine acres, built in a series of layered effects, on a sloping hillside. It has an Egyptian Avenue, entered through iron gates under a magnificent Pharaonic arch, and a beautiful Circle of Lebanon, built round a cedar tree dating back to 1693.

There is room for 30,000 graves in the main part of the cemetery, at a cost of £2.10s each. It was opened in 1839 and is regarded as London's most fashionable necropolis. Where more fitting, therefore, for the body of a man who in life owned one of the largest mansions set in one of the most fashionable locations?

The coffin is carried from the hearse to the newly dug grave, watched by the group of male mourners, women not being present at an actual internment, as they are considered too emotionally fragile to attend. Both of Barrowclough's sons are at the graveside, though, supervised by a house servant.

And so the body of James William Malin Barrowclough is laid to rest in the main part of the cemetery, alongside many far more illustrious individuals: George Wombwell (d.1850) the menagerie owner, F. W. Lillywhite (d.1854) the cricketer, and Lizzie Siddal (d.1862) wife and muse to Pre-Raphaelite poet Dante Gabriel Rossetti to name but three.

(At the time of Lizzie Siddal's burial, Rossetti was so overcome with grief that he placed the manuscript of his poems into her coffin. Later this year, he will return to Highgate cemetery, where he will arrange for the coffin to be opened, as he is no longer quite as grief-stricken, and so desires the manuscript back.)

****

Leaving these scenes of death and burial, we move on to life and art and the small artistic colony known as the Transformative Brotherhood, who are busily putting the final touches to their various works in preparation for their first major exhibition. The preparations take various forms. Alice Mor, sculptress, is working on the head of a young woman. It is based on a Classical Greek goddess. She has paid various visits to the British Museum, made drawings, and is now attempting to replicate what she observed in clay, using a variety of palette knives.

In the back parlour Marcus Carrow, sketcher of London night life, is putting the finishing touches to his triptych. Upstairs, Edgar Jerrold is etching London Street Scenes as fast as he can etch, while in the next room, Hans Holker's watercolour scenes of Wapping and the Docks are proceeding apace. Meanwhile Walter Hugo Hunter has appropriated the front room for his personal use and is busily turning out a series of gritty urban paintings depicting the contrast between the magnificent new city streets and structures and the passing population, especially the homeless and destitute. Sewers, railways, smoking chimneys, order and chaos all jostle for space on his canvases.

They are disquieting pictures, as far removed from the anodyne aestheticism of the Pre-Raphaelite Brotherhood's work as night is from day. But they do share one characteristic: the Pre-Raphaelites used models they found in the ordinary workaday world that existed outwith the rarefied atmosphere of their studios. So Hunter has used Flitch and Liza, the workhouse escapees, in many of his canvases.

Here they are posing under a streetlamp, looking malformed and undernourished as they watch a parade of red-coated soldiers marching by. Here they are again, bare-headed ragged street children, singing to a crowd of top-hatted gentlemen and ladies in silk crinolines who are ignoring their plight. There are also a couple of striking portraits of Liza, in a selection of curious bonnets and paisley shawls, staring straight out of the canvas with her tiger eyes.

There is an upside to all this for the brother and sister. Thanks to their new roles as artist's muses, Flitch and Liza now have access to regular meals, and permission to doss down on their fur rug in a warm place by the kitchen stove. Of course, their good fortune is not without its downside too. To be at the beck and call of Hunter means long hours posing in various rundown locations, and their new benefactor is not above losing his temper and throwing the odd paintbrush at their heads.

A couple of recent temperamental outbursts have resulted in the two youngsters staging a walkout, and Alice, who has grown fond of Liza, has had to play mediator and go-between. One way and another, it has been an illuminating learning curve for all concerned; the Brotherhood have learned that being in possession of an artistic temperament is not an excuse for bad behaviour and Flitch and Liza have learned that they actually do have the power to change their circumstances, albeit in a limited capacity.

While all this hive of artistic activity is taking place, the agent hired to arrange the exhibition is engaged in various tricky negotiations with the owner of the department store playing host. Mr. John Gould of John Gould & Company, 'Never Beaten on Price', sees the whole event in a very different light to the artists, who envisage it as a serious occasion whereby the general art-viewing public will be faced with the reality of life in the city for so many of their fellow citizens. Paintings of real London people, not clouds, countryside scenes and women artfully posed, languorous and inviting or cold and corseted. And once their social consciences have been aroused and enlightened, the visitors will hopefully purchase the canvases to hang on their walls.

Mr. John Gould, however, envisages the event as an occasion to show how very modern his store is by staging an art exhibition by controversial young painters. He also envisages exploiting it to display the variety and popularity of his department store, using the art exhibition as a lure. Especially since a rival, a Mr. Lewis, has recently opened a department store in the same street, also promising keen prices and the ability to match any competitor.

With these outcomes in mind, a pianist playing a selection of popular tunes to accompany people going round the exhibition has been suggested, but rejected. A display of drawing room furniture to 'go with' the paintings has met with a similar response. Ditto the idea that one of the artists might like to set up their easel and do lightening sketches of members of the public ('people would love to have a memento of their visit, especially a nice sketch of their children') was treated with eye-rolling contempt.

Life might imitate Art, except when it comes up against the face of commerce. Finally, after days of to and fro negotiations, a compromise is reached. A space will be made for the exhibition near, but not too proximate, to the restaurant, thus allowing patrons to view the artworks in silent contemplation, and then partake of refreshments (to the accompaniment of light background music).

"Look, it's that or nothing," their agent tells the Transformative Brotherhood wearily. "I've done my best but at the end of the day, it's his department store. At least you have a space. Admittedly it's not the Royal Academy but it's a start. And other venues around the country can be arranged. It's quite the done thing now for exhibitions that start in London to travel round other major cities. Imagine your work hung in Manchester, or one of the other big industrial towns ~ people up there would really appreciate what you are trying to say."

Put like that, and with funds at rock bottom, Art relinquishes its purist principles and higher intent and grudgingly gives way to commerce. And so, on a Sunday morning, while church bells summon the faithful, the obedient and the hopeful to worship a deity in whose existence the Transformative Brotherhood have little belief, a covered wagon draws up outside their lodgings, and is speedily filled with the work of their hands. The cart sets off for Oxford Street, followed by members of the group carrying such implements as hammers, tacks, hanging cord and small cards with their names and the names of their various works.

****

But before the doors of John Gould & Company open on Monday morning to admit visitors, it is high time to catch up with the lone figure we last saw making his disconsolate way from the graveyard where his wife was buried to the great city where he hopes to find his two children. Arriving in London, Sam Thomas has spent every succeeding hour and day since we left him in a desperate search for his lost loved ones.

All day long he tramps the streets, peering into passages and doorways, diving into derelict courts, inquiring of passers-by, sitting atop omnibuses as they clop their way along the London streets. In his heart he knows that his actions are futile. The proverbial needle and haystack have nothing on his quest, but he cannot cease.

Every evening, as the city empties out, instead of laying his weary head on his pillow, he joins the other nocturnal ambulants, trekking between densely dark alleys and brilliantly-lit squares as the night wears on, with the moon and clouds sailing up high above him.

Feral children stare and bare their teeth at him as he passes their doorways and alleys. Occasionally he is greeted by a night constable patrolling his beat. Chimes from church steeples bisect the night hours. He hears dogs barking, drunks singing, couples quarrelling. Sometimes, he sees strange and puzzling things ~ a man determinedly pushes a squeaky wheelbarrow along a deserted street at 2.00am, its contents wrapped in what looks like a burial shroud; a woman in a nightdress stands on the balcony of a big house waving her arms to the moon and singing. Eventually day appears coldly, looking like a dead face out of the sky.

All the while, the sands of time are running swiftly away. His ship is now berthed and awaiting its passengers. His search is proving to be futile. But sometimes, at the very last minute, just when all seems utterly hopeless, Fate decides to throw out a lifeline. After another fruitless night tramping the cold inhospitable streets, Sam Thomas is so exhausted that he is forced to sit down in a doorway to rest. Which is where he is discovered, fast asleep, a few hours later by a handsome young woman with deep blue eyes and hair the colour of untamed treacle. She carries a leather work satchel, and her face bears a keen and interested expression.

The doorway marks the entrance to a terraced house. The number of the house is 122A Baker Street, and a brass plate to the right of the bell announces that one of the businesses located here is that of L. Landseer, Private Consulting Detective.

Miss Lucy Landseer (for it is she) regards the occupier of her doorway with head askance and a slight frown upon her alabaster brow. His clothes do not mark him out as one of the many derelict street people who spend their lives sleeping rough. She bends closer: he seems to be breathing. A hopeful sign. She continues her observations (a good detective always uses her eyes first before drawing any conclusions). She smells no drink. She sees no signs of blood, bruising or torn clothing.

The stranger's presence is therefore a bit of a puzzle. She is about to step carefully over the man and enter the building to begin her day, when he suddenly awakes with a start, his eyes opening wide when he spies her standing in front of him. Jumping to his feet, the man stumbles out of her way, uttering bewildered apologies for his unexpected presence. Lucy Landseer notes the American twang in his voice. She responds with an acknowledgement and a gesture suggesting that both his presence and apology are of no concern. The man stares at her for a few seconds. Then his gaze shifts and fixes on the brass plate.

"Excuse me, ma'am, do you know anything about this L. Landseer? Is he any good at his profession? Only I have a problem, and it strikes me right now, seeing his name up there, that maybe a detective could be just whom I need to help me out."

Lucy Landseer steps up to the door of the building, then turns and looks at the man. She smiles. This is very familiar territory. Since she started her business as a female consulting detective, she has endured many such mistaken identities. If the mistaker is male, they do not remain long, which is why her entire clientele so far has been female.

"I am Lucy Landseer, private detective. If you would care to accompany me, I'll take you upstairs to my office. Then you can tell me about your problem. If I can aid you, I will. If not, I may be able to offer you some good advice," she tells him.

Briskly, she leads the way across the black and white tiled hallway and up the stairs, where she unlocks a door on the first floor. It is labelled Consulting Room. She glances over her shoulder. To her surprise, the man has followed her. Lucy shows him to the gold painted clientele chair, padded with crimson velvet, because first impressions and the comfort of clients is important.

She unties her bonnet and places it and her winter coat on the peg behind the door. Then she stations herself behind her desk, which is placed in front of the portrait of some female worthy who has no connection with her business whatsoever but adds an air of verisimilitude to the enterprise. She leans forward, cups her chin in her hands and regards the man attentively.

He stares back at her, mutely. She reads the distress in his eyes.

"I can send out for hot rolls and coffee, if that would help?" she suggests. "I presume you have not breakfasted?"

He nods. "I am sorry, ma'am ... miss?"

"Landseer," Lucy supplies.

"I don't mean to be impolite, Miss Landseer, ma'am. Forgive me. Only I have never encountered a female private eye before, if you understand me."

You and practically everyone else in this city, Lucy thinks wryly. Her current status as the only consulting female private detective in London has come about via her previous career as a freelance writer. A novel featuring the glamorous Belle Batchelor, private detective, and her faithful canine sidekick Harris, proved so popular with the reading public, who wrote to her publisher in droves requesting help with their various problems, that the decision to practice the profession she wrote about was a logical step.

She bestows a sympathetic smile upon her visitor, then summons the young woman paid to clean the building and the rooms and run errands. A short while later, she enters bearing a covered basket which she sets down on Lucy's desk.

"Now, Mr. Thomas, please help yourself," Lucy says, having managed to elicit a few of her client's personal details from him while they waited.

After breaking his fast, Sam Thomas wipes his mouth on his coat sleeve. Then he sits back in his chair. He clears his throat. Lucy's pen hovers over a clean page in her notebook, waiting. Haltingly, and with long pauses while he struggles to get control of his emotions, Flitch and Liza's father spills out his story in raw gobbets of sorrow and distress.

Lucy listens, writes, thinks that all the fictional plots in the world have nothing on what she is hearing: A breadwinner who sets out for a faraway land, determined to make life better for his family. A family divided by a vast ocean. Letters that went unanswered. Money sent that certainly never reached its recipients. Finally, the long voyage back and the discovery that the family home had been knocked down and the family scattered to the four winds. Then the visit to the Union Workhouse and the awful revelation that his wife was dead and his children had vanished.

Once the tragic tale is finally told, the teller lapses into silence, head averted, eyes fixed upon the carpet. Lucy sets down her pen, and, picking her words with care, asks, "Have you thought of placing an advertisement in some of the daily newspapers?"

Sam Thomas lifts his head. "No, I hadn't, and now it is too late. My ship sails on the evening tide."

"But it is not too late," Lucy tells him. "For an advertisement can be placed at any time. All one needs is a box number. And someone to call in at the newspaper office at regular intervals to check it. I can do that for you, Mr. Thomas, if you so desire."

His face brightens. He nods. "It was a lucky day when I ended up on your doorstep, ma'am. If you'll take over my search, I'll make sure you are well paid for your pains. If you find my children, the sky's the limit ~ you can ask for whatever you like."

Lucy demurs. "My fees are set, Mr. Thomas. A little extra for expenses is all I need. And an address in New York where I can write and let you know how I progress with my investigation. I promise you I shall leave no stone unturned. If your children are here in London, I will do my utmost to find them for you."

Sometime later, Lucy Landseer leaves her consulting room and catches an omnibus. In her satchel is a letter of introduction to a city bank and a banker's draft for a sum that will cover her fees and expenses for the near future.

In her brief career to date, Lucy has exposed one bigamous husband, aided a distraught wife to escape the prison of her miserable marriage, and revealed two unscrupulous dowry hunting scoundrels. Nothing is beyond her powers of deduction. If Frederick and Eliza Thomas are anywhere in London, wherever they are in London, she will find them. Yes indeed. Of that she is quite, quite sure.

****

Meanwhile, Detective Inspector Stride sits behind his desk at Scotland Yard, contemplating the pile of paperwork that has miraculously appeared over the weekend. Where does it come from? More to the point, why has it all ended up on his desk? He picks up the first report, which appears to be some directive from the Home Office. Pen-pushing mandarins with no idea how a real police service works, he thinks disgustedly, filing it straight to the bottom of the pile.

An hour later, after many expletives and considerable refiling, the report has worked its way to the top of the pile again. Stride stares at it, frowning. He vaguely recalls reading it. Or did he? He sighs, signs his name at the bottom of the report to indicate he has read it, even though he is pretty sure he hasn't, then summons a constable, who is instructed to take all the reports and place them on the head of Scotland Yard's desk. If in doubt, move the paperwork onwards and upwards.

Stride is just contemplating his next move, which may involve a mug of the treacly black brew that passes for good coffee in his opinion, when there is a quick knock at his door and one of the junior constables enters.

"Beg pardon sir, but Inspector Greig says could you come. There's been an incident at Highgate Cemetery."

Stride feels his heart sink. The conjunction of 'incident' and 'cemetery' usually means only one thing: a grave has been disturbed or a body has been taken. Even though times have moved on from the days of the resurrectionists, the crime of opening newly dug graves and stealing any objects buried with the recently deceased is still an ongoing problem. Wearily, he gets up and fetches his coat and hat from the peg. Whatever has occurred, somebody is going to have to inform some grieving family that their loved one's remains have been dug up or interfered with, and the chances are high that the somebody will have to be him.

He orders the constable to whistle up a cab and when it arrives, sits glumly staring into the middle distance until it draws up at the ornate iron gates to the cemetery. Telling the driver to wait, Stride alights, to be greeted by Greig and a couple of gravediggers armed with spades and apprehensive expressions.

"I was alerted to the event early this morning by the constable who patrols the area," Greig says, drawing Stride to one side and speaking in a low voice. "The grave in question belongs to Mr. James William Malin Barrowclough. I have to say I did wonder whether his death would be the end of the matter. It appears my speculations were correct."

Exchanging significant glances, the two detectives traverse the wide gravelled path, following the cemetery workers, until they reach a newly dug plot in the main part of the grounds. Stride halts by the graveside.

"We buried a coffin in this grave yesterday," one of the gravediggers tells him. "Now look at it. Someone's been and disturbed it."

Stride stares down. He frowns. "I don't see ..." he begins.

"When we dig a grave, after the coffin has been lowered in, we backfill the earth round it and make a nice smooth top. This ain't a nice smooth top as we'd leave it. It seems like the earth has just been flung onto it any old how. It looks wrong."

"Wrong?" Stride queries.

"Definitely wrong," his fellow grave digger nods. "Flat on top. Wrong shape altogether."

"I see," says Stride, who doesn't really. "So what are you suggesting has happened?"

"Could be giant moles?" a third grave digger suggests but is immediately quashed by one of his companions.

"There's no such thing as giant moles. Nor mermaids in the Thames what sings Rule Britannia, nor giant pigs running amok in the sewers. Now, be told."

The gravedigger lapses into silence. They all stare fixedly at the grave mound without speaking for a while. Then, "Right, lads, let's get digging," the first grave digger says briskly. "And if you Scotland Yarders would like to stand over there, we'll call you when we've finished."

****

Across town, Miss Lucy Landseer alights gracefully from an Atlas omnibus and makes her way up Ludgate Hill. Eschewing the windows of the numerous jewellers, hatters, shawl-sellers and pawn brokers that line either side, she reaches, eventually, a small gateway that leads, via a maze of alleyways, unpaved courts and lanes strewn with rubbish, cats and noisy children, to Fleet Street, known throughout the capital as 'the Street of Ink'.

She is heading for a small square off the main thoroughfare. It contains two trees, currently leafless, behind some iron railings, and a building with a black painted door containing the words: '*Illustrated London Express*' in bright copper lettering.

Lucy has had cause to visit the archive of this edifying newspaper before, in her professional capacity. It advertises itself as 'the social conscience of the Londoner' and errs on the side of lurid and dramatic stories. Preferably with pictures to match. The editor subscribes to the 'more blood, more interest' school of journalism.

In the past, Lucy has supplied the paper with various stories and articles of a slightly racy nature, and as a result now has free access to the basement, where back copies of the newspaper are kept. Today she hopes to glean inspiration from former articles of lost and found children. Maybe some hints on how to structure an advertisement and proceed in her investigation as well.

She greets the elderly porter on the door, states the nature of her visit, and makes her way down to the basement, where the leather-bound back copies are kept. Steeling herself for what is always the trickiest part of the visit, Lucy approaches the desk at the centre of the room, behind which the newspaper's elderly archivist, indexer and Keeper of The Catalogue, Armand Malpractis, is at work.

"Good day, Mr. Malpractis," she greets him in a brisk 'we have been here before; you do know who I am' tone.

Malpractis starts. He peers up at her over the top of his spectacles. His expression is one of surprise mixed with cautious doubt. Lucy can almost see the cogs in his brain starting to whir as he attempts to place her into one of the many thousands of categories in the card catalogue of his mind. (Young woman: Consulting detective: Private.)

"Ah. Yes. I see. You are here again, aren't you?"

Lucy agrees that she is indeed.

Malpractis takes a pencil from behind his left ear, a feat that involves unwinding it from a lock of his long grey hair, and draws a series of small, interlinked boxes on a cream card. "You are here once again in your official capacity, I presume?"

"I am. I wish to find out whether there have been any stories of lost children being discovered. Or advertisements on that theme. I hope you can help me."

Malpractis fills in the centre box. He frowns. "You wish me to consult The Catalogue?"

"I do. If it is not too much trouble."

"I see. You do. Yes. Ah." He rises to his feet, giving her another quizzical glance. (Trouble: female inquiry.)

Lucy knows the form. Silently, she follows him at a suitable distance to the large dark wooden cabinet containing the drawers filled with index cards, each linking a subject to the relevant article or page in the back copies of the newspaper. The Catalogue is a holy object, to be consulted only by its high priest and treated with the reverence accorded to some religious relic.

Malpractis opens a drawer and begins to riffle through the cards, muttering to himself: "Children … births of … farming out of … crimes against … crimes committed by … deaths in infancy … education of …

employment of ... yes ... ah ... this might be of interest. And this. Indeed."

Lucy tiptoes over to one of the desks. She knows from experience that, at this point, she has become extraneous to proceedings. Now, all she can do is wait for Malpractis to transfer his mutterings to slips of paper and then line them up with the relevant bound volumes. She opens her satchel and extracts her notebook. Turning to a clean page, she writes: Lost Children. Then she sits back to await the outcome.

****

Back at Highgate Cemetery, detectives Stride and Greig are standing at the edge of what was, until very recently, the last resting place of Mr. James William Malin Barrowclough. Now, all that remains is an empty coffin. The grave diggers, their work completed, lean on their spades, watching the two men's reactions.

Greig purses his lips. "So much about this man has been a complete mystery. The snow figure, the blackmail parcels. At one point, I admit I was almost prepared to close the case and accept that his death was a most unfortunate accident. But in the light of what we recently learned from our French visitors, and now this discovery, it seems that somebody is going to the most extraordinary lengths to ensure that he disappears completely from the face of the earth."

Stride glares at the grave diggers. "How has this happened?" he demands. "I thought the gates to the cemetery were locked overnight."

There is a shuffling of municipal feet. "Well, sir, it's like this," one of the men finally says, "It being Christmas and all, things got a bit lax, you might say. And then a couple of the men decided not to come back after the Christmas holiday ~ it's miserable, hard, back-breaking work digging a grave in the cold, especially when there's a heavy frost. So, the locking of the gates got left to whoever was the last man to leave. Only nobody was ever sure they were the last man to leave, given the size of the place. So sometimes the gates never got locked. Sir."

"I see," Stride says grimly. "So, thanks to your incompetence, anyone could come in and remove a body. As they clearly have done. I shall be writing a very stiff letter to your supervisor. This is not good enough. Not good enough at all."

He turns away from the empty grave. "No point hanging about here any longer. I suggest we return to Scotland Yard and arrange to send a couple of men round to the usual hospitals to see if a body answering Barrowclough's description has been handed in for dissection. And then one of us will have to go to the Hampstead residence and inform the grieving widow what has occurred." He pauses, waiting for Greig to volunteer for the job. He doesn't. Mentally gritting his teeth, Detective Inspector Stride leads the way back to the main road to find a cab. He has a feeling that it is going to be a long and difficult day.

****

By contrast, Miss Lucy Landseer has spent a long and profitable morning reading back copies of the newspaper and making notes. It is surprising how many children go missing every week in London. Some run away, some get abducted, some just vanish from their homes for no conceivable reason (according to their parents). Then again, others are found or unexpectedly turn up, occasionally imposters claiming to be the scions of recently dead parents who have left wills with unclaimed money. She mentally makes a note to watch out for this.

At one o'clock Malpractis indicates that the library will close for an hour. Lucy gathers up her belongings, gives him a bright smile and heads out into the briskly busy streets. She has garnered enough to move on to the next phase of her inquiry: drafting an advertisement to be placed in the most popular newspapers. She decides it must be done prudently using a box number, so that she can weed out unlikely applicants. But first, there is somewhere she needs to visit. And some individuals she needs to consult before she places her advertisement.

Later that evening, after she and the man she shares a house with have had supper, and the pots have been washed and dried, Lucy decides to broach the subject that is at the forefront in her mind. She wishes to pay a visit to Cambridge, to speak with the people who knew and looked after Fletcher and Eliza. The description given to her by their father lacks current details. Lucy does not want to be inundated with letters claiming to be from or about the two runaways. Nor does she want a string of imposters turning up to claim the reward. She needs to know the intimate details that will identify Fletcher and Eliza Thomas precisely.

Lucy's man is a professor at the university, so provides her with information about trains, good places to eat her luncheon, and the location of the Union Workhouse. An offer to accompany her on her excursion is sweetly turned down. Lucy knows her own powers of persuasion. She will achieve her goal better on her own. People are more likely to answer probing questions when the asker is female. Mainly because they don't expect her to be asking them.

Later, as she sits writing up her notes, her professor regales her with the tale of one of the fusty old-fashioned dons who simply could not come to terms with the new influx of female students. "He arrived at the lecture room one morning, to see only a row of women students sitting at the back. Apparently, he glanced round, and then said, out loud, 'Well, as there is clearly nobody here today, I shall not be able to deliver my lecture' and walked out!"

They both laugh, but Lucy thinks inwardly that if she ever met this man, she would not hesitate to give him a piece of her mind. The foolishness of him! The following morning, she writes a polite, but official, letter to the overseer of the Cambridge Workhouse, expressing a wish to ascertain certain facts from him relating to two former child inmates who have recently left. She is careful to give away as little as possible and makes sure she signs the letter L. Landseer.

The response comes back promptly, and thus, on a bright day that holds out the first real promise of spring, Lucy Landseer steps down from a station cab and walks boldly up to the forbidding door of the Union Workhouse. She is greeted by a bald man with a frill of red hair around the lower part of his skull. We have encountered him before. On this occasion, he has shed the apron, in deference to the visitor, but his small blue eyes regard her with the same hostile suspicion as they did Flitch and Liza's father, when he appeared on the doorstep.

Undeterred, Lucy introduces herself and proffers her card. "I am here on behalf of my client, Mr. Sam Thomas. I believe he visited here and has spoken to you. My client is no longer in this country and in his absence, has charged me with ascertaining the whereabouts of his two children, who recently left this place. We believe they may have made their way to London."

The overseer's expression passes from astonished to suspicious via truculence. "Well, for a start, Miss … they didn't leave, they ran away. And as such, they ain't the responsibility of this h'establishment any more. No. And so I told your 'client', as you call him, when he came here making the same inquiry."

Lucy is unperturbed. "Indeed, you did. But what my client failed to get from you is an exact description of the two children. He only remembers them from when they were much younger, you see. They will have changed, and before I can begin my search, I need to have a clear image in my mind of what they look like today. This is the purpose of my visit.

"I hope you will be able to furnish me with such a description, which will enable me to eliminate any children who are presented to me, but do not match the actual description." She pauses, smiles winningly, "You see, my client is now a wealthy man, and is able to offer a substantial reward to the person who can lead him to the recovery of his lost children."

She lets the words 'substantial' and 'reward' hover in the air and waits patiently for them to land.

"How much are we talking about here, miss ...?" the overseer asks, his tone suddenly changing to a more mollifying one.

Lucy looks off, "As I said, substantial. I am not in a position to discuss the actual amount. It will be paid only when the two children are found and to the person who finds them. Now, can you help me?"

The naked greed in the man's small blue eyes is almost comical. "I see. Yes. Well, in that case, if you wouldn't mind following me to my office, miss, I shall fetch my dear wife, as she was the one who looked after the girl ~ like a mother to her, she was. Nothing too much trouble. I can furnish you with a description of the lad myself."

Lucy follows him and then waits until the man returns, accompanied by a slatternly middle-aged woman, her hair escaping from an untied bun. Her face is as hard and unyielding as that of her husband. Her small pebble-grey eyes regard Lucy coldly.

"Mr. Farish says you want a description of the girl Liza Thomas. Is that right, miss?"

Lucy affirms that it is.

The woman continues staring at her. "O'course, my memory ain't what it used to be. Might need a bit of something to help it along, if you understand me, miss, times being what they are." Brazenly, she holds out her hand, palm up.

Lucy does indeed understand her. She opens her purse and tips some coins into the palm. Her face is as expressionless as she can make it. Her soul seethes inwardly. The woman thrusts the money into her apron pocket. "Ah, well now. That's better. Great promoter of memory is a bit of money. Now then, what can I tell you about the girl?"

Lucy gets out her notebook and writes down everything the man and his wife say. When they have finished, she rises, thanks them with as much courtesy as she can muster, given her disgust at their mercenary attitude. She refuses a cup of tea and is shown to the front door with much bowing and scraping from the workhouse overseer, who has clearly decided she is now to be flattered and fawned over.

Shaking the dust of the awful place from her heels, so to speak, Lucy sets off towards the station, deciding that a good walk is what she needs to take the nasty taste of the two grasping workhouse employees out of her mouth and from her thoughts. Her respect for Sam Thomas and her determination to track down his missing children has just been given even further impetus by the time spent in that desolate building.

It is said that walls have ears. If so, then the walls of the Cambridge Union Workhouse are privy to a certain conversation that happens after Lucy Landseer, fortified by tea and crumpets, is back on the train to London. The conversation takes place in the comfortably furnished private back parlour and is between the unpleasant overseer and his equally unpleasant partner.

It goes like this: "I always said those children were trouble from the moment they arrived," the overseer says. "Remember the fuss they kicked up when they had to leave their ma? And the boy had a way of looking at me. Didn't matter how much I beat him he'd keep on with that face. Staring me down as if I was the one in the wrong."

"The girl was no better," his shrewish spouse responds. "Ooh, she was a sly one. You'd give her a job of work and next minute, she was nowhere to be found. Kept trying to break into the women's section to look for her ma."

"It's my view that we deserve every penny of that reward for what we had to put up with from them two."

"I agree. But how are we going to get our hands on it, that's the problem?"

"I been thinking about that, my love. You have a sister, don't you? Runs a public house in London, I believe. Maybe it's about time you paid her a visit. The parish owes us some time off. I think your sister is about to suffer a serious accident ~ one that means her nearest relative has to go and nurse her back to health."

The woman nods slowly. "And you'd have to come with me, coz I ain't going to make the journey all the way to London on my own. Wouldn't be proper at my time of life."

"That's exactly the way I'm seeing it."

"But London is a very big place, innit? How'd we begin to find them?"

"I thought of that too. What we do, see, is the moment we arrive, we tell the police that we were looking after the boy and his sister out of the goodness of our hearts as they were orphans. And they repaid us by stealing all our life savings and then legging it. Lay it on thick, we will. Make sure you pack your oldest clothes ~ we don't want them to think we're anything but poor people.

"That way, we'll have every policeman in the city on the lookout. Save us tramping the streets ourselves. We won't mention any reward, nor that some private detective, or whatever she calls herself is also looking for them. Once they are handed over to us, we take them round to her and collect the reward. After we've punished them for causing us so much trouble, that is."

There is a pause. Husband and wife stare into the fire, their faces alive with avarice as if already seeing the golden fruits of their plan in the bright flames licking the coals.

"Well, when all's said and done, it's no more than we deserve. When shall we start for London?" the woman asks.

"You write to your sister, and I shall write to the Board of Guardians. As soon as the Board gives us permission, we will be on our way."

****

Enough! Let us now leave this scene of sordid sophistry and pass lightly on to more exalted matters. And here are Art and Commerce joining hands and combining their efforts in the newly opened first exhibition of the Transformative Brotherhood. Here is a gallery space hung with paintings. Here, just a step away, is a well-appointed restaurant offering morning coffee, light luncheons and teatime delicacies.

Everything possible has been done to make sure that the carriage and pavement trade are aware that John Gould & Company are once again seizing the branch of innovative retail and shaking it vigorously. There are men with sandwich boards patrolling Oxford Street. There have been full-page advertisements in the newspapers. There are even some members of staff dressed up as 'artists' in smocks and berets, waiting to greet customers as they step through the gold and glass doors, and steer them towards the escalator that will conduct them upwards, to the Elysian fields of canvas and cake.

There has been a great deal of interest from the London public, to whom anything new is always worth investigating, even though in this case, there's no blood or bodies. Gratifyingly, a few of the paintings have already been sold, though so far only the ones that feature Liza, who has been described in various art magazines as 'a beautiful young street dweller with tiger eyes'. Both Flitch and Liza are not sure about this at all, given that they have never dwelled on a street in their lives, nor encountered any tigers while not doing so, but they have been reassured by Hunter that there is no such thing as bad publicity.

And now, events that seem totally disparate and unconnected, are suddenly about to collide, as often happens in Babylondon, the greatest city on earth. The exhibition has been running for a week when it is visited by Monsieur and Madame Avignon, who have been buying final souvenirs of their trip to London and have decided to regale themselves with a cup of the strange English brew called tea (because when in England, this is apparently what one does in the afternoon). As usual, they are accompanied by their valet Plouc, who functions today as general factotum and parcel carrier.

After refreshing themselves with 'the cup that cheers but does not inebriate' and a plate of assorted cakes, they pass from the restaurant to the display of paintings. In the matter of Art, Monsieur and Madame consider themselves true connoisseurs. After all they hail from

Paris, the centre of the Art universe, where Art is made on every street corner.

The Avignons live and breathe Art. When they finally shrug off this mortal coil, the word Art will be found engraved upon their hearts. Or running through their veins. Possibly both. Thus, they peruse and pose and consider and comment their way round the exhibition, with Plouc struggling along in the rear, trying not to drop any of the parcels but periodically failing.

At last Monsieur and Madame finish their critiquing. They are now ready to return to the hotel, to finish packing, before catching the train down to Dover. But wait! What is this? Plouc has come to a halt in front of one of the pictures. He has dropped his parcels and is jabbing a finger excitedly at the painting. Alas, Monsieur and Madame are unaware of Plouc's antics, as they are strolling towards the escalator, deep in conversation. Plouc looks round wildly, spots Alice Mor sitting placidly behind a desk, marking up a catalogue, and makes a beeline towards her.

"*Mademoiselle, je vous en prie: ecoutez: çe monsieur!*" Plouc says, gesticulating over his shoulder in a slightly manic fashion. "*Je l'ai vu. C'est lui, l'homme à la gare! Oui. Je suis sûr! C'est lui!*"

Alice Mor shrinks back in her seat, raising both her hands in a fending off manner. "I am sorry, I do not understand what you are saying," she says, speaking slowly in a 'talking to the hard of understanding' voice.

Plouc repeats himself, upping the hand gestures. She frowns at him. Then, to her horror, he leans across the table, grasps her by the sleeve, and starts shaking it. "Venez avec moi, mademoiselle. Venez, venez vite!"

Without thinking and too shocked by this unexpected attack upon her person by a complete stranger and a foreigner, Alice Mor stands up and follows him over to the triptych. Plouc digs in his trouser pocket, produces a folded piece of newspaper and carefully unfolds it. The headline says: **Underground Railway Claims Another Life** and shows a picture of a man in an overcoat and top hat falling in front of an oncoming train. Plouc gestures at the picture.

"Ce n'est pas un accident. Cet homme ..." he points at the bearded man in one of the panels, *"c'est lui qui a tué le monsieur! Vraiment, mademoiselle."*

Alice Mor scrunches up her face. She vaguely grasps what the earnest young foreigner is saying. But ... it is too wildly improbable. Isn't it?

"I think I understand you," she says at last. "But I don't know what you want me to do about it."

Plouc dances up and down excitedly on the tips of his toes as his mind frantically tries to remember the words he requires to communicate to this young woman. In the end, he launches into what he hopes is a mime of a constable, though to Alice's eyes it could just as easily be a circus clown.

"No, now I don't understand you," she says.

Plouc digs deep, trying to mine the few words of English he has mastered. "Tell ... Scotland police?" he says.

"I?" Alice Mor opens her eyes wide. "But why me?"

Plouc nods vigorously at her. Then he thrusts the newspaper cutting into her hand. "I go at France now," he says simply as he spins on his heels and hurries off after Monsieur and Madame, leaving Alice Mor staring from his departing back to the triptych, then to the article and shaking her head in bewilderment.

Later that day, after the store has closed, and Alice Mor has returned to the shabby house she shares with the rest of the Transformative Brotherhood, she regales them with her strange encounter with the exotic young French visitor and shows them the cutting. They listen enthralled.

"I say, Mor," Marcus Carrow exclaims, "Fancy that, eh? I painted a murderer! That's one for the newspapers. That'll pull in the crowds. I reckon we can raise our prices considerably on the back of this."

Alice Mor demurs. "I'm not sure we should take the young man seriously. Maybe I misheard. Perhaps he was mistaken."

"Doesn't sound like it," Carrow counters. "If you want my opinion, you should write to Scotland Yard ~ that's who he was talking about. And do it as soon as you can. Because once this gets out, everybody is going to want to buy the triptych, I guarantee. After supper, I am going straight up to my studio to produce some copies."

Alice Mor looks to her husband for his take on the matter. He agrees. "Go ahead. Invite them to come to the exhibition. Or better still, to come here. Marcus can bring his sketches to show them and tell them about the night he made them."

"Good idea," Hunter agrees. "And while you're washing the pots, tell Eliza that I want her to sit for me tomorrow. I need my 'girl with the tiger eyes' for a few more paintings. Bless the day I found those two urchins! They are going to make my fortune."

Sighing, Alice Mor begins to clear the table. "If you all think that is the right course of action, then I'll write later tonight."

She carries the plates down to the kitchen, where Flitch and Liza are peacefully eating their supper at the table. As she stacks the dirty pots and cutlery in the sink, and sets the kettle to boil, she tells them all about the funny Frenchman and his strange tale. Alice Mor has her back turned as she speaks, and so she doesn't see the worried expressions flitting across their faces.

That night, with Alice Mor's letter written and dispatched, the two youngsters bed down on the floor by the warm stove. The kitchen is dark, except for the shaft of flickering light from the gaslamp out in the street. The house is quiet, all abed. No words have been exchanged between them. They do not need to confer. They know what they have to do.

****

It is early next morning, before the sun rises and a thousand chimneys fill the air with smoke, and here are Flitch and Liza leaning on the parapet of London Bridge, contemplating the grey, sluggish water, the craft already plying up and down the river, and their future.

They are barely recognisable from the underfed workhouse inmates who arrived illicitly in the city aboard a London coach. Regular meals have brought colour to Liza's cheeks, and her hair shines like copper flames. Flitch seems to have broadened at the shoulders. Their faces have filled out. Their skin is less grey in tone and more healthy. Both are wearing warm clothes, albeit second-hand. They have boots that fit, and possessions tied up in two small bundles.

"It's been alright here, hasn't, Liza?" Flitch says, his eyes following the wake of a coal barge as it heads downriver. "Except for the paintbrushes!"

The girl stares into the middle distance. "I'm going to miss Alice. She was good to me. Do you think she'll miss us?"

"Bound to. But it's time to leave. We can't risk getting involved with the p'lice. They might reckernise us and take us back to the workhouse."

Liza agrees. "Will we see Alice and the others again?"

He shrugs. "Maybe. When we've had a few more adventures."

She nods. "Main thing, we're together, Flitch. I don't want us to be apart again."

The boy puts an arm round her. "Never going to happen, Liza. I'll always look after you. Promise. You and me together for ever." He holds out a crooked index finger. She links it with her own.

"You and me for ever, Flitch."

The rising sun streaks the water with golden rays as the two figures shoulder their small bundles and cross the bridge. They pause at an early morning coffee stall for coffee and slices of buttered bread, then having broken their fast, they set off once more, walking away from the dark sprawl of the city, following the road to wherever it will take them.

****

Meanwhile, over at Scotland Yard, detectives Stride, Greig and Williams are facing the grim reality that once again they have reached a dead end in their investigation. The word 'dead' being extremely pertinent to their current position. No body matching the description of Mr. James William Malin Barrowclough (deceased) has been furtively handed over at the rear entrance of any of the London teaching hospitals.

The river police have reported no bodies answering a similar description being fished out of the Thames at the usual locations where dead bodies are accustomed to wash up. They have put Information Wanted posters up in all the main police offices, but so far no one has come forward to identify the bearded man on the platform who allegedly pushed Barrowclough in front of the train.

Stride is particularly put out by the situation. He stares down gloomily at yet another set of goading headlines accusing the Metropolitan Police of being unable to find their own backsides without a map and compass (*The Inquirer*). Other newspapers speak of the double grief of a widow who has barely come to terms with the demise of her life-partner, only to be faced now by the disinterment of his still-warm body (accuracy never being the press' strong suit), and its subsequent disappearance into thin air.

None of this is making good reading and neither Stride nor Greig are feeling good about reading it. They stare down at the headlines. Stride frowns, muttering something about haystack and sewing implements. Greig sucks in his breath. Young Williams opens his mouth, then closes it again. Greig raises an eyebrow. "You have something to say, Tom? Spit it out, man. God knows we could do with some fresh ideas."

Detective Constable Williams fiddles with the top button on his jacket. "We can't find a man or a motive. So maybe we need to find something else."

"Find what?"

Williams stares into space. "Perhaps we'll know when we find it," he says elliptically, staring into the middle distance.

Stride snorts. "Well, as long as it doesn't involve any more Johnny Frenchmen. What a waste of time he was. Good British detecting. That's what we need here. Boots on the ground. If we ever want to get to the bottom of this blasted investigation."

****

Meanwhile Flitch and Liza's walk has brought them, via grimy terraces and assorted churches to the outskirts of the city, where coal merchants jostle with scrap yards and weed-strewn plots awaiting development are filled with standing pools of black water. London, it appears, doesn't end, it merely dilutes itself, awaiting its next incarnation.

They walk on. Time passes. The road bends, straightens, then bends again. They lose their sense of direction. Eventually, a hundred different tones of a hundred clocks of a hundred local churches together with the grumbling of their own stomachs brings them to a halt. They have walked for hours; they seem to have walked for miles, although in actual fact, they've merely gone in a wide arc and have now come to the end of Commercial Road and reached the Docks.

They halt. In the distance they see the tall masts of ships rearing up into a smoky sky. The sight draws them like a magnet. They scurry down a narrow street fringed by cheap lodging houses and reach the foreshore. Here are tiers of shipping, for the broad highway of the river is almost blocked, with merely a narrow pathway of grey, glittering water left open in the middle.

There are Spanish schooners and brigs and a crowd of foreign vessels, with huge lighters waiting beside the wharf. Beyond them, a dense grove of masts rises up from the water, thick as giant reeds and filmed over with the grey mist of vapour rising from the river, so their softened outlines seem to melt into the sky.

"Is this the sea?" Liza breathes, her eyes wide.

"Don't know. Might be," Flitch answers.

"It's magic," Liza says. "Just magic." And she stares and stares until it feels as if the tall, masted ships and the lapping water has filled her from head to toe. "I could stand here all day, Flitch, just looking."

Flitch smiles. He watches some barrels being rolled down a gangplank, then glances round and spots a riverside tavern, the swinging wooden sign proclaiming it to be The Ships Head (naturally). "Them boats will still be there after a spot of dinner, Liza," he says kindly, taking her arm. "Let's go and get a bite to eat."

The Ships Head is old. Very old. Outwardly it looks as if it has been sunk and retrieved from the murky waters of the Thames many times in its history. The wooden outer barge boards are rotten, paint peeling off like an elderly dowager at the end of an evening. The first floor hangs drunkenly over the footway. The rooftiles are crooked and broken. It oozes age and decay. Shakespeare could have drunk here, maybe Marlowe or Ben Johnson, though only if they were absolutely desperate.

The two youngsters enter the bar. The public house smells familiar. Their nostrils pick up odours of unwashed flesh, faeces and overcooked food, with the addition of the cold stench of the Thames. They look around. The predominant interior colour, from the walls to the drinks to the people is greyish brown. Total silence falls as they advance from the door towards the counter across what seems like a long distance. Every eye is fixed on them.

Eventually, a huge man with long greasy hair tied back in a ponytail rises from one of the tables. He seems to occupy more space than physics should allow. He regards the newcomers thoughtfully, his hands tucked under his canvas apron; his glance not missing a single detail.

"Yers, young sir and madam? How can I help you?" His voice has the husky timbre of one who has been smoking strong shag tobacco from birth.

Liza slips her hand into Flitch's. He squeezes it. Then he steps up to the man, a swagger in his step. 'Two rounds of ham sandwiches and two bottles of ginger beer, if you'd be so kind, my good man. Not too much mustard on the ham." he adds, staring the big man out.

There is a pause. The landlord throws back his head and laughs. "Well said, young shaver. Aren't you the bold one! I like the cut of your gib. You go and sit in that booth over there and I'll get my good lady wife to bring over your food and drink."

Flitch and Liza edge into the empty booth. The clientele, having surveyed them thoroughly for anything interesting or possibly transferable, go back to eating and drinking and banging their fists on the tables. After a while, a short surly woman with hard eyes and a thin mouth like a whip slaps two plates of sandwiches onto the table, before bringing two glass bottles of ginger beer out of her apron pocket. Flitch pays her and they tuck in. They are ravenous after their long walk, so the stale quality of the bread and the fatty nature of the ham is barely noticed. The ginger beer is cold and refreshing.

"Can we stay here a bit longer?" Liza asks, as they leave The Ships Arms and head back to the foreshore.

"Whatever you want, Liza," Flitch replies. "I see there are lots of lodgings to be had. We can spend a few days looking around, no problem."

They are just about to head upriver, when a dark-skinned man suddenly rushes round the corner, pursued by three other men, all brandishing sticks and clubs and shouting, "Stop thief!" A crowd of sailors, wild-eyed drunken men in cloth caps and low-browed, brawny-armed women follow after, shouting their support for the thief or thief-takers.

Flitch and Lisa cower in a nearby doorway, waiting for the hubbub to die down. Then they hurry across a small bridge, passing barges, black with coal and timberyards crowded with yellow stacks of deal until they reach streets of poverty-marked tenements, with half-naked children playing in the gutters. Flitch stops outside a ships' chandlery, with pea-coats, waterproof overalls and sou'westers hung on poles outside. Bidding Liza to stand by the wall, he enters, emerging a short time later. He beckons Liza to follow him. They stand by a quay, seagulls screeching overhead.

"Look," Flitch says, "I bought one of these." He shows her a small horn-handled knife with a shiny sharp serrated blade.

Liza's eyes open wide. She hefts the handle of the knife. It feels warm to the touch. "You never had a knife before," she muses.

"Didn't need one before," Flitch says. "It's for having, not using. Just in case." He slips the knife into his pocket and takes her arm. "Right, let's go and take a look at some more big ships. Then we'll get some supper and find a place to sleep."

They set off along a towpath. On one side, the bank is lined with distilleries, gasworks and all sorts of factories with chimneys of preternatural dimensions. Everything is on a gigantic scale. On the other side they pass a tier of huge steamers with gilt sterns and mahogany wheels. A group of yellow-skinned men carrying wicker baskets hurry by, chatting and gesticulating in a strange language. Liza's eyes open wide. "There are so many foreigners," she breathes. "It's like we ain't in England anymore."

The rest of the day passes in sightseeing and marvelling. Evening falls, and the lights come on in the many waterside taverns and coffee houses. Fiddle music and song can be heard from invitingly open doors. Grog shops and dancing saloons open, prepared to welcome customers. Brightly clad women emerge from their daytime lairs and take up various positions on street corners. Flitch and Liza buy a poke of fried fish pieces from a stallholder and perch on a convenient bollard to eat it.

"You know what," Flitch says, "maybe there are ships here that are going to America."

They sit silently contemplating the thought, turning it over, exploring it.

"I should like to see one of them ships. Then I could think of it sailing over the sea to where our Pa lives," Liza says.

Flitch crumples up the empty paper poke and tosses it into the dark water. "Tomorrow, we'll go and find a ship that's going to America and you can take a good look at it. Now let's go and find somewhere to sleep."

While the two youngsters settle down for the night, their minds full of boats and sailors and faraway lands across great oceans, two visitors arrive at The Ships Head. They are welcomed by the landlord and his wife and shown into the parlour, where a good fire burns. A nice hot supper of chops and some porter is offered and enjoyed, for the journey down to London on the train and then across it in an omnibus has exhausted them both.

While they eat, and in between the landlord and his wife making periodic trips to check on the bar, family news and gossip is exchanged, the ruinous price of everything is discussed along with the many and various ways of eking out victuals and drink so as to get the maximum profit. For publicans, like workhouse overseers could be said to be in the same line of work.

Later, as they climb the stairs to their room, the overseer of the Cambridge Union Workhouse mutters to his wife, "tomorrow, we'll visit the police and see what they have to say."

And so, night falls on ship and shore.

****

Dawn breaks, bringing with it a letter. The letter is placed before the desk sergeant, who, after frowning over the 'To whom it may concern at Scotland Yard' superscript, decides to take it and place it on Detective Inspector Stride's desk, on the basis that if it contains a complaint or a problem, the further it is from him the better.

Thus, it is Stride who opens and reads Alice Mor's carefully penned letter regarding the strange young Frenchman and his startling information. Deciding he hasn't got any more time to spare for Johnny Frenchman, Stride moves the correspondence on to Greig's desk, where it is eventually read and taken seriously which is why, some time later, Detective Constable Tom Williams, accompanied by two local beat constables, finds himself stationed opposite the alleyway leading to the Cat & Cauliflower public house.

Day slides into dusk. Dusk slips into twilight, a twilight made even more opaque by the streetlamps, which have not been lit. The only light comes from the pipes of the local policemen, who have spent the past few hours working on every sort of joke about why Williams, an officer from Scotland Yard, is hanging around on a dodgy street corner waiting for a couple of tarts to appear. He is young, good looking, so they are happy to disbelieve his explanation.

Twilight slips into night. The two accompanying officers get bored and decide to resume their beat, given that nothing is kicking off in this neck of the woods. Williams stamps his feet and decides that a bit of a warmup by the fire and a small drink might be allowed.

He cuts down the narrow evil-smelling side alleyway and enters the public house. Even though it is mid-week the queue at the bar is three deep. Some small children sit under tables. Dogs growl at each other and lap up spilt ale. The air is thick with the fug of cheap tobacco and stale beer. A couple of men are sitting at a crusty table, engaged in a heated discussion about the ownership of a cabbage. Or it could be a carriage, it is hard to make it out.

Williams joins the back of the queue at the bar. A few men eye him suspiciously. Not local, their glance says. Therefore, not welcome here. Gradually, he works his way to the front of the queue, where he encounters Sad Ginge sitting on the counter looking cross. A nice juicy fat rat, caught earlier in the festering alleyway has been rudely taken off him and sold to a man with a greasy cloth cap and a terrier pup to train.

Williams orders a small drink, and idly scratches the cat under its chin. He likes cats. He grew up with them. Sad Ginge finds unexpected comfort in the caress and purrs throatily.

"Blimey, young cove, you're a lucky 'un. That cat'd take your fingers orf if the mood took him," the landlord remarks, passing a damp cloth over the bits of the bar unoccupied by Sad Ginge.

Williams seizes the moment. He leans forward. "I'm looking for a couple of young ladies," he says, adding hastily, "not for the reasons you think. I am a police officer from Scotland Yard, and we need their assistance in solving a crime. Have you seen any of these individuals in here recently?"

Tom takes a small artists' sketchbook from inside his overcoat. He flicks it open to some drawings showing a heavily bearded man and a young woman, then the woman and a female companion. The landlord screws up his eyes, holding the drawings up to the dim lighting and frowns.

"If people are gonna come in here droring my customers behind their backs, I might haveter charge them," he grumbles.

"Do you know who the young women are?" Williams persists.

"Might do. Might not. You get all sorts in here. It's a popular venoo, as the French say. Why d'you want to know again?"

This is like wading through treacle.

Tom closes the sketchbook. "We are trying to track down the man in the sketches."

The landlord sucks in his breath slowly. "Are we now. Well, he ain't a regular in this pub, I can tell you that."

Sad Ginge gets to his paws and still purring, moves to sit closer to the young detective constable. He looks up at him with a world-weary expression.

"What's it worth?" the landlord says, eyeing Williams.

"It's worth not having the local police and the weights and measure inspectors coming down and checking you don't water the beer," Tom says. It is only a guess, but the change in the landlord's expression tells him it is a lucky one.

"Alright. That's Moll Marryat and her sister Poll. They rent a room on the second floor."

"Are they there now?"

The landlord shrugs. "Might be."

"I would like to go and see. Any objections?"

Another shrug. "I ain't their keeper. Round the side of the bar and through the door on the left."

Williams follows the instructions. The stairs are old and treacherous. There is no light, but when he reaches the second floor, a thin strip of candlelight is coming from under one of the two doors off the landing. He knocks gently. There is no reply. He knocks once more.

"Who's there?" a woman's voice says.

Tom Williams tells her his name. There is a pause, then a rustling sound from within the room and the door is opened a crack by a very young woman. Her fair hair is dishevelled, her eyes sleepy, her shoulders carelessly covered by a soiled wrapper.

"Can't a girl have a night off, for god's sake?" she complains. "Right, I suppose you can come in. Three and six. Money on the nightstand before we do the business."

Blushing, Tom Williams explains his true purpose. The girl hears him out in silence, winding a stray blonde curl around her finger.

"Let me see the drawings," she says when he has finished speaking.

Tom shows her the sketches. She studies them intently.

"When did you say he was here?"

He tells her. She bites her lower lip as she tries to remember. "Yeah, I think he was one of mine. He had a funny way of speaking, as I recall."

"Foreign?"

She shakes her head. "Could've been from up north somewhere. Not sure. Not London, I'm sure of that."

"You didn't happen to ask him where he actually came from, by any chance, or for his name?"

She regards him with sly amusement. "Er … no, I didn't. Coz I'm not in the business of serving tea and cakes and p'lite conversation. Funnily enough. Now, I've told you all I remember, so if you're sure you don't want anything else …?" she cocks her head on one side saucily, grinning at his obvious discomfort.

Tom Williams backs away from the door, bidding her a hasty goodnight. The door closes and he retraces his steps cautiously back down the treacherous stairs, crosses the public house floor and walks out into the street.

As he makes his way to his lodgings, Williams reflects on what he has been told. He recalls Mr. Greig remarking that Mr. Barrowclough, the deceased man, spoke with a slight northern accent, which he tried to hide. And now the man associated with his demise has been revealed to have a northern accent too. There is no such thing as a coincidence ~ how many times has he heard Mr. Stride saying it? A coincidence is just an explanation waiting to happen. That was what he said. So tomorrow, he will take the coincidence, and set about finding the explanation.

****

But what of that other investigation ~ the one being pursued by the indomitable Lucy Landseer? Here she is now, making her way to the offices of one of the newspapers where she has secured a box to receive any replies to her advertisement. Lucy steps up to the front desk, gives the box number and waits. So far, she has had only two letters in response. Both were vague in content and lacking the information that she knows will identify the real Fletcher and Eliza Thomas. For Lucy is not a fool ~ she has laid a trap to reveal any fake children who might be proffered to her by parents, guardians or bogus members of the public after the reward.

As she waits for her box to be searched, Lucy thinks about Sam Thomas. She really wants to telegraph him with good news. She recalls his desperate face, the sadness in his eyes as he described visiting the grave of his dead wife. So much tragedy encapsulated in one small family. Surely there must be some reparation for such suffering? Despite being a child of the manse, Lucy does not believe in God any more ~ she is too much a pragmatist, nevertheless she cannot help sending a silent request to a deity she has turned her back on long ago that something good might happen. Soon.

The newspaper clerk reappears, carrying a letter, which he hands over. Lucy signs for it and thanks him. She glances at the superscript as she walks out. Green ink? A lot of elaborate curly bits round the edges of the envelope? Not what she was expecting. Intrigued, she heads for a small discreet restaurant that caters for ladies out on their own. She orders tea and toast. Then she slits open the letter and reads the contents.

****

Richard Cuthbert, of Barrowclough and Cuthbert, land agents is a man with a problem. The unexpected demise of his partner has left a huge hole in the business ~ a hole that he is currently unable to fill. Nobody (apart from his good self) knows how to bully a prospective client into selling their land at an advantageous price to the company. Nobody could draw up a land agreement with clauses so meandering and vague that the client always appended his signature without bothering to question what exactly he was signing up to. In this, as in so many aspects of the work of Barrowclough & Cuthbert, his partner reigned supreme.

Now, he is faced each morning with an empty office, an unoccupied chair, the future sprawling ahead, unplotted and unschemed. No wonder he is in a grumpy mood. And his day is about to slide sideways even further. A knock on his door heralds the arrival of Detective Constable Tom Williams, the light of pursuance in his eye.

Wearily, Richard Cuthbert waves him to a chair. "Yes, officer?" he says flatly. "How may I be of assistance to you today?"

Williams extracts a notebook from an inner pocket and a pencil from another one. He leans forward, his gaze focused upon Cuthbert's face. His stance is that of a greyhound straining in the slips. "I am hoping you can supply me with some background details to your former partner, Mr. James Barrowclough," he states.

Cuthbert frowns. "Background details? Why? The man is dead, isn't he? 'An unfortunate accident' I gather.

An unfortunate accident leaving my company facing potential ruin."

Undeterred, Williams continues. "Scotland Yard has not closed the files on the case. We still have unanswered questions. Your cooperation would be much appreciated." He pauses. "You have not received any suspicious parcels addressed to you personally, have you?" he inquires, his face a mask of total innocence.

Richard Cuthbert stiffens. His eyes widen as the implications hit him. "Why? Do you think I may be about to? Is that what it is about? Someone has a grudge against the business and is picking us off one by one? My God! I have a wife and four children! Are they going to be threatened by this madman also? Heaven forfend!"

Tom Williams does not respond. He sits still, recalling what he has been taught by his colleagues about allowing the silence to ask the questions for him. (Imagine a tap with a drop of water forming at the spout. You wait while it elongates, gets bigger. Wait until it is almost ready to fall. That's how long it can take). So he waits. Seconds pass. The clatter of the typewriters and Cuthbert's heavy breathing are the only sounds to be heard. Then Cuthbert swallows. "Very well, I will try to help you, officer. What do you want to know?" he says hoarsely.

The interview over, Tom Williams sets off back to Scotland Yard, only pausing on the way to refresh himself with a mug of coffee and a slice of bread and butter. In his pocket are several pages of useful information about James William Malin Barrowclough (deceased). Finally, a new line of inquiry has opened up. He strides through the doors of Scotland Yard with his head held high and goes straight to his shared desk to write his report.

Later that day, Williams shares his findings with Lachlan Greig. The senior detective reads through the report, his brows contracting in a frown. The younger man waits, hands behind his back, trying to stifle the memory of his former schooldays, and the caning he usually received in similar situations.

When Greig has read to the final sentence, he nods thoughtfully a couple of times. Then looks up. "This is a very thorough piece of work, Tom; you are to be congratulated. I have read it with interest. So, just to make sure: you think the death of Mr. Barrowclough and the events surrounding it have their origins in something that happened in his past. And you want my permission to explore these past events. Is that correct?"

Tom Williams nods. "Mr. Stride says people kill for three main reasons: self-preservation, revenge or loyalty. If we can understand why this man went to such lengths to torment Mr. Barrowclough before murdering him, we can hopefully reassure ourselves that he will not strike again. The widow and her two children will not become future targets of his hatred."

"Do you think we can catch him?"

Tom bites his lower lip. "That I cannot say, Mr. Greig. But in my opinion, we have to try. A man has lost his life. Surely we should do everything we possibly can to bring his killer to justice?"

Greig studies the young man. His dark eyes spark intelligence and honesty. Greig recalls the first time he encountered young Tom Williams, a lowly beat constable with more education and intelligence than was normally the case. He used words like 'amiss' in his reports; he could punctuate. And he didn't begin every sentence with 'I was proceeding'.

He also had a fine sense of injustice ~ indeed had it not been for the encouragement of his colleague Detective Sergeant Jack Cully and his good wife Emily, young Williams might have been lost to the Metropolitan Police. The young man was prepared to sacrifice his career for the sake of a stalled investigation. If he disallows him his head now, Greig muses, will we lose him again?

"So, what do you have in mind, Tom?" he asks. Then he sits back and listens as the young detective constable outlines his proposal. And when he has finished explaining his strategy, Greig drums his fingers on his desk for a while, staring at the copperplate writing of Williams' report and finally reaches a decision. "You are owed some leave, aren't you Tom, as you worked over the Christmas and New Year period? How about taking it now? That way, I don't have to account for your absence to Detective Inspector Stride. Keep a written record of any expenses you incur and send me daily reports of your progress. And good luck."

Greig stands, indicating that the meeting is at an end. His eyes shining with enthusiasm, the young detective constable scrambles to his feet and shakes his hand. "I won't let you down, Mr. Greig. Thank you for trusting me with this."

I sincerely hope you won't, Greig thinks, as the door closes behind his colleague. He settles back into his chair. He is taking a risk letting a young and largely unproven officer loose on what might be a fool's errand. He hopes it will be worth it.

****

For Flitch and Liza, their adventures in dockland are progressing apace. They have found cheap lodgings in a small side street. They have stood on a quayside and watched a huge ocean-going vessel slip its moorings and edge quietly out into the main channel of the river, on its voyage to New York. And here they are now on a cold crisp morning hurrying across a bridge suspended on iron chains. They turn down a flight of winding steps where at the bottom they discover a line of little wooden houses with the words 'PAY HERE' inscribed on them.

There are passengers waiting to board a line of boats moored at the pier. There are men in uniform with bands around their hats bearing the inscription L.&W.S.B.C, which a man explains to the youngsters stands for the London and Westminster Steamboat Company. The air is full of cries of 'This way for Cremorne', 'Anyone for Lambeth or Chelsea?' 'Who's for Hungerford?'

Flitch edges them to the head of the queue, purchases two tickets at a booth, then holds Liza's hand as together they step onto the first boat, which immediately sets off, shooting through the bridge, and leaving behind the usual proportion of passengers who have just paid for their tickets in time to miss it.

Flitch and Liza head for the front of the boat and secure a prime position by the rails. The boat chugs upriver passing barges black with coal on one side, and timberyards stacked with yellow deal on the other.

"This is a fine adventure, Flitch," Liza cries, as the steamer shoots noisily under Westminster Bridge, and, after a lot of shouting of 'Ease her!' 'Back here' is manoeuvred to a temporary halt at Westminster Pier to allow passengers to disembark.

Having shed its passengers, the boat pulls away from the pier, turns and dashes through one of the arches of the bridge. It forges on, seagulls shrieking overhead, under a pale smoky sky, past boat-builders' yards, the yellow-grey stone turret of a neighbourhood church. For a brief while, their nostrils are assailed with the nauseating stench emanating from the bone-crushing establishments that line the south bank, then this gives way to distilleries and all sorts of factories, their huge chimneys spewing smoke into the air. They pass gasometers and potteries ~ everything is on such a gigantic scale that they feel like small insects trapped on a floating island. Liza slides her hand into her brother's hand. He squeezes it reassuringly.

Eventually the boat returns to its moorings. Canvas and rope and tar, the stench and din of the river give way to the smell of spices and coffee and small boats pushing off continually from neighbouring stairs, while men standing in their sterns wriggle through the river traffic by working the scull behind, like a fish's tale.

"That was prime," Flitch says as the two make their way back to their lodgings. "Now, you have a bit of a rest, Liza, while I go and earn us some money."

Flitch takes a pack of worn playing cards from his jacket pocket and shuffles them. While in the workhouse, he learned various card tricks from the male inmates ~ the foremost one being Find the Lady. It was a way of passing the time. He's been playing for years. He is good. The best. Flitch has noticed how the seamen, especially the Chinese and Lascars like playing chess and cards and other games with small, coloured tiles. He has also observed that they like to bet.

There are plenty of empty crates lying about. It doesn't take him long to set himself up with a playing surface and an upturned bucket to sit on. He gets out his cards and does an elaborate shuffle. The cards arc in the air and fall into a neat pile.

"Here's the Queen of Hearts," Flitch announces. "Now look closely ... where's she gone?" In no time he's drawn a crowd of Oriental seaman, only too willing to put down money to show the scrawny English boy that they can 'find the lady' with the best of them. But they won't. The queen is up his sleeve. The money is in his pocket.

While Flitch and his sister have been enjoying the sights and sounds of their river trip, the overseer and his wife have not been idle. Waking early in their fusty bedroom over the bar, they descend to the back quarters of the public house to break their fast. It has been decided to let the landlord and his wife into the real reason for their visit, on the basis that the more eyes there are, the better the chances of pocketing the reward. Not that the reward is actually going to feature in the narrative. Blood might be thicker than water, but money makes the world go round.

Over buttered toast, eggs, ham and milky tea, the tale is told. But an unexpected corollary emerges, mine host has seen the two miscreants! More, they have been in his pub. They ate some ham sandwiches. He takes the visitors into the bar and points out the actual booth the boy and his sister sat in.

"I remember them two partickler coz the boy was a bold 'un," he says.

"That he certainly is," the overseer agrees. "And the girl is a lazy little slut. Never finished her chores. Always where she shouldn't be. They gave us a mort of trouble. And then they scarpered, taking all our savings and the wife's jewellery."

The overseer's wife assumes a doleful expression and clasps her doughy hands to her bosom. "Our ma's pearls," she says, casting a quick sideways glance at her sister. "They took our ma's beeyootiful pearl necklace wot she left me in her last will and testitute."

"The vile varmints!" her sister exclaims. "The only thing of value wot she had in her whole life."

The landlord clicks his teeth. "If I'd of known, they'd have nivver left the premise," he says, shaking his head. "So, what's yer plan?"

The overseer outlines the action he intends to take. The landlord and his wife listen and nod. "I shall get my regulars to keep an eye out," the landlord says, "chances are they've left the area, but you nivver know."

You never know indeed. After a visit to the local police office, where Inspector Beare of K division is appraised of the situation and promises are extracted that his men will be on a sharp lookout for two runaway thieves, the two workhouse employees saunter back to the Ships Head for a pub lunch, to be followed by a pub snooze upstairs. After which they leave the Ships Head for a walk around the docks, keeping a watchful eye for the two runaways.

They are just returning to the public house for a cup of tea and a biscuit or three when they turn the corner and see a little crowd of loose-robed, pig-tailed individuals crowded excitedly around something. There are red-turbaned Lascars in the crowd as well. The air is full of strange words and stranger gestures.

The overseer's wife clutches her husband's elbow. "Foreigners. I don't like the look of them," she says. "They might just put the Evil Eye on us. Let's hurry."

"Ain't nothing to be afeard of," the overseer says scornfully. "They won't hurt us."

Nevertheless, they edge cautiously round the outskirts of the group, both averting their eyes, and return to the Ships Head as fast as they can. Meanwhile Flitch collects his playing cards, dismantles his equipment and, pockets full of coins, sets off to find Liza and show her his winnings.

Later, when the boats are all tied up for the night, and candles glow in the portholes, Flitch and his sister make their way back to their lodgings. Their bellies are full and their hearts light as they wind through the street, for a great ship has just docked and the crew have come ashore seeking pleasure and pastime.

Liza sings the refrain of a music hall song. Flitch struts and jingles the wealth in his pocket. And then, suddenly, out of the blue, a heavy hand is laid on the boy's shoulder and a familiar voice says: "Gotcha, my fine fellow me lad!"

Flitch twists and struggles, but the overseer (for it is he) has him in a vicelike grip. "Oh no, you ain't going nowhere!" he sings out, as he clamps the boy's arm behind his back and begins to haul him along the road, kicking at the back of his legs to make him go faster. A few passers-by watch curiously, but don't interfere. You don't get involved with fights in this neighbourhood. Not if you are wise and want to hang on to body parts, or your life.

For a split second, Liza is rooted to the spot. Then she launches herself at the bulky figure, screaming and hammering him with her fists, but it is no use. The man is much taller and far stronger. He brushes her off as if she were a fly. "Flitch!" she yells. "Don't leave me!"

The boy glances back, reading the horror in her eyes. "Run, Liza!" he commands, as his captor drags him relentlessly towards the door of The Ships Head. "Run, and don't stop. Never stop. Don't be afraid, I'll find you. I promise. One day, we'll be together again."

****

It is a long journey from the rough and ready world of the Docks to the secluded and wooded environs of Hampstead Heath. Even further if measured in social terms. Here, in her muslin-curtained bedroom in Hill House, with the blinds still half drawn, the widow of the late and not much-lamented James William Malin Barrowclough sits at her dressing table contemplating her reflection in the glass.

It is said that some widows suit mourning ~ black enhances their fragile femininity. It is also said that there is nothing in the world that so evokes pity in the masculine breast than a fair young widow dressed in black. In Helena Barrowclough's case, alas, the only sentiments likely to be evoked in any breast, male or female, are that of bewilderment that this collection of small bones can actually walk about.

Despite visiting Peter Robinson's Family Mourning Warehouse with her sons, where she was measured for a watered silk gown, a velvet gown and accompanying hats, gloves and mantles, all in the latest French style, and all in the deepest black imaginable, the impression conveyed to the sympathetic onlooker is of a stringy fowl. The sort you'd buy to boil down for stock. Helena's pallid face is beginning to line. The black emphasises it. If she leans forward, there are great hollows between her collar bones. Her nose sticks out like a chicken's beak. Her cheekbones recede from it. Her eyes are dull. Her thin wrists emerge from the plain black sleeves, blue-white and bony.

She extracts a number of lethal looking jet hairpins from her bonnet, sticks them back into it and tosses the bonnet onto the silken counterpane of her single bed. She has returned from a short walk on Hampstead Heath. Just recently, she has found herself ensnared by fits of restlessness. Hill House feels oppressive. Unexpectedly, she requires different air in her lungs. It is as if after all the years of lying abed or resting on a sofa, she has suddenly decided to open the cage she kept herself imprisoned in.

Walking also helps her to order her thoughts, which she now needs to do. After visiting the family lawyer, where the contents of her husband's Will have been made known to her, she finds there is a great deal to think about. In a dry factual voice, as if reciting a railway timetable, the lawyer informed her that her late husband has made provision for the boys' school fees. That was to be expected.

However, as for the rest, it seems that she must shift for herself. Contrary to appearances, her husband was not nearly as wealthy as she was led to believe, mainly by him. The money she brought to the marriage went long ago. Everything else, including Hill House, is tied up in the business. And then there are debts from private speculations and enterprises that failed. Gambling and horse racing debts. And somebody called Mrs Katarina Aspinall at an address in Maida Vale, to whom a sum has been left 'for services'. She does not want to think about that.

So, the shifting must begin. She must retrench. The house has already been put on the market. Creditors must be paid out of the sale. She has her eye on a small cottage in the village of Bray, where she can live simply and be close to the boys. She glances at her tiny watch. The servants will be gathering in the dining room. A woman on her own does not require an army of male and female servants, two cooks, an outside boy, a gardener and a coachman. Let alone a stable of carriage horses and an old former nanny whose grip on reality is fading fast.

She must gird her loins, screw her courage to the sticking point and go downstairs. Unpleasant news has to be broken. The sooner she starts breaking it, the sooner she can get on with whatever remains of her life. Helena rises, rearranging the black skirt. She crosses the floor of the room, suddenly struck by the thought that she has not cried. Not when the policeman came and told her of the accident. Not when the body was lying in its coffin in the parlour. Not on the slow procession to the chapel. Not when the detective with the world-weary eyes came to inform her that the body had vanished from its final resting place. Not even when faced with selling the home wherein she was born and grew up.

Ah well. She opens the door, deciding that after she has sacked most of the staff, she will order supper for herself. She thinks about a roast bird, in butter sauce. Fresh vegetables, soft white bread. A glass of white wine followed by a creamy dessert. Her mouth waters. She could eat it all twice over. How strange, she muses, as she descends the staircase, slowly and carefully, for she is still getting used to it, how very strange that the unexpected loss of a husband has been replaced by the unexpected acquisition of an appetite.

****

Midnight. The hour when ghosts stalk the land. A man approaches the gate of Hill House and tries to open it, but the gate is shut and padlocked. He peers through the bars. Sees the 'For Sale' sign appended to the front door, and the wooden shutters pulled down, sealing off the interior of the house from prying eyes.

The man stands at the gate, his eyes riveted on the deserted mansion. It is so quiet he can hear his own breathing. An owl hoots in the distance. Small creatures in the undergrowth go about their nocturnal activities. Trees rustle in the night wind. For a long time, he doesn't move. Then, with a long, exhaled sigh, he turns his back on the silent dwelling and walks away, taking the winding path across the lonely heath.

****

Meanwhile, back at The Ships Head, the capture of Flitch is being celebrated in fine style. The board positively groans with boiled beef, potatoes, greens and an apple tart. Gin and beer flow like running water. Not that the captive is dining on such riches. Or dining at all. Locked in an attic room where old furniture and lumber is stored, Flitch sits on the dusty floor, his head in his cupped hands. His clothes are torn, the money in his pocket removed, his knife confiscated, and he has a big bruise on the side of his head from being whacked by the overseer.

Flitch is in total shock. His agile brain, so adept at coming up with ideas and solutions is currently unable to process his sudden change of circumstance, and as a result he cannot think how to proceed. There is a small, barred window set high up in the wall, through which wan slices of light fall upon various trunks shrouded in blankets and sacks. In the semi-darkness they seem to loom in the corners, like fearsome dead things.

To distract himself, he gets out his pack of cards and begins to shuffle them, more as a way of calming his nerves. He tries to recall what they said when he was dragged into The Ships Head. The police were mentioned. He's sure about that. And punishment. That was said too, by her, the hard-faced cow. And of course, they wanted to know where his sister was, but he didn't tell them. He'd never tell them. They could threaten him all they wanted, they could beat him black and blue, they could break every bone in his body: his lips were sealed.

Flitch's hands move automatically in the darkness, shuffle, shuffle. Where's the lady? Who knows? Where's the knave? Locked away in the dark. Rain starts pattering on the small window. He hears it as if from a great distance. Then he hears it pattering down the chimney. And suddenly, Flitch is on his feet, the cards in his pocket, and he is lifting bags and pushing aside trunks until he has cleared a way to the fireplace.

He kneels down and slowly inches his head forward, into the empty grate. He twists his neck and looks up. At the end of a dark tunnel above his head, he can see a pale moon shining. A few raindrops fall onto his upturned face, like tears from the stars. He stretches his arms up into the chimney, then eases his head and shoulders into the space beneath them. His hands feel around, find some protruding brickwork to hold on to. Flitch grips the brickwork as hard as he can and begins to haul himself upwards towards the night sky.

Luckily for Flitch, the Ships Head is one of the last remnants of a bygone era, when chimneys were built wider than today. Also lucky is that the landlord is too mean to light fires in the first-floor bedrooms. Nevertheless, his knees and elbows are scraped raw, and his throat filled with dust and soot by the time he has squeezed out of the top of the chimney and lowered himself onto the roof below.

Flitch perches atop the slate ridge and coughs out the contents of his lungs. Then he looks about him. He has never been so high up in his life. If he stood up, he could reach out and almost touch the bright stars overhead. Below him, he sees the twinkling lights of the ships' topmasts. He lets the rain fall onto his face, occasionally wiping it with his jacket. He shudders to think what a sight he must look. If Liza could see him now, even she might not recognise him. He sends out a silent message that wherever she is, she stays safe until he finds her.

From his rooftop vantage point, Flitch sees the first streaks of dawn arriving, and realises that even though he is high above the street, it only needs one person to look up, and he could be in danger. Time to descend and find an elsewhere to be. He swings his leg over the ridge and lowers himself slowly down the side of the roof until his hands are able to grip onto a gutter and his feet find a windowsill. From there, he edges carefully sideways until he reaches a downspout. Then it is an easy sliding descent to the street.

As soon as his feet hit the cobbles, Flitch takes to his heels. He runs until he can run no more. Wheezing and gasping for breath, he leans against a convenient wall. He is bruised, battered, filthy dirty, and bone-weary. Also, he has no idea where on earth he is, but at least he is free.

We left the indomitable Lucy Landseer opening a letter penned in green ink. Let us now return to her to see what she found therein. The letter comes from a Mr. Walter Hugo Hunter, Urban Artist. It is Mr. Hunter's belief that he may know or possibly know or perhaps might have known the two young persons of whom the inquirer seeks information. (Not only is Mr. Walter Hunter's writing difficult to make out, but his style is equally curly and convoluted). The upshot of the communication is that should the inquirer wish to ascertain whether the two persons are the same ones that Mr. Hunter thinks they are or might be, the inquirer should call at an address in Camden Town whereupon, if the inquirer makes himself known by the production of this missive, Mr. Hunter will endeavour to satisfy him as to the veracity of his suggestion. Yours, etc etc.

Well! Lucy reads the letter through a second time. At first, she thinks it is a scam. Then she reconsiders. Previous letters had focused mainly on the reward. This letter makes no mention of it at all. From a third reading, she gets the impression that the writer will only divulge the information once he has assured himself of the validity of the seeker. This is promising. She decides to seize the moment (a favourite expression of her father's) and pay the verbose Mr. Hunter a visit.

A short time later, the Islington omnibus deposits Lucy in Camden Road, where, after making several inquiries and a misdirection, she eventually finds the address of Mr. Hunter. Lucy stands on the unwhitened step and knocks with her fist on the shabby door, which is opened by a slightly harassed young woman wearing a long shapeless gown in a colour best described as wilted cabbage. She has men's shoes, and a paint-spattered apron. At the sight of Lucy, her face falls. "Oh dear. You aren't the man with the clay, are you?" she asks.

Lucy agrees that she is neither a man, nor a bringer of clay. She informs the young woman she has come to see a Mr. Walter Hunter and produces the letter for the young woman to see. The young woman runs her hands distractedly through her hair, causing several small combs to clatter to the floor. "He has just stepped out for a short while."

"I am happy to wait," Lucy smiles, winningly.

"Oh. Are you? Well, I cannot say when he will return." She stops, stares hard at Lucy. "Is this about Flitch and Eliza?"

Ah. Lucy feels a surge of triumph. Her advert never mentioned the names of the two youngsters. It was her first test to see whether she was being lied to. "I am inquiring about them, yes."

"But wait ~ Walter said … but you are a …"

"A woman. Yes. My card." She hands over one of her business cards. The woman's gaze travels from the card to Lucy. "A female private detective? I have never heard of such a thing before." She pockets the card, hesitates, then opens the door and stands back. "Please come in, Miss Landseer. You must take us as you find us, though. We are a colony of artists and makers and we do not always hold to the accustomed standards."

Lucy enters the hallway, sidling past several canvases propped against the walls. The air smells of turpentine, glue and paint. From upstairs comes the sound of rhythmic hammering and the odd curse. The young woman glances up towards the sound and pulls a face. "Maybe we should go down to the kitchen?" she suggests.

Lucy follows her. "Tea?" the young woman suggests, nodding her towards a chair. Lucy says she'd love a cup.

"I'm sorry, I don't know your name," she says, sitting down.

"I'm Alice Mor. I'm a sculptress. That was my husband you heard. I apologise for his language. He's struggling with some frames. We have an exhibition in town. It's proving hard work."

Lucy accepts a cup of milkless tea. "Thank you, Mrs Mor. As I said, I have come about the letter I received from Mr. Hunter."

"Are they in some sort of trouble?" Alice Mor asks, sitting down on the opposite side of the table.

Lucy shakes her head.

"Only we thought when they ..." Alice Mor begins, then presses her lips together.

"You thought?" Lucy suggests gently. "What did they do?"

"I think you should wait until Walter returns, Miss Landseer. It was he who wrote to you after all. To be honest, my husband counselled against it. After all, we did not know whether whoever had placed the advertisement meant them good or meant them harm." She eyes Lucy suspiciously over the rim of her teacup. "I still don't know, so I shall say nothing more until Walter returns. Some more tea?"

Lucy likes her tea milked and sugared, but she doesn't want to chill the atmosphere even more, so she accepts a second cup, allowing it to cool at her elbow. A change of subject is called for. "Please tell me about your work, Mrs Mor," she smiles. "You said you were a sculptress, I believe? I have never encountered one before. May I see some of your work?"

Alice Mor unbends a fraction. "I can show you some photographs, if you like," she says. "My current pieces are all in the exhibition."

"I should love to see your photographs," Lucy says, putting what she hopes is the requisite amount of enthusiasm into her voice.

"Then I shall fetch them." Alice Mor rises and walks to the kitchen door. Lucy hears her footsteps going up to the ground floor. Then silence. She suspects that Mrs Mor has gone to tell her husband all about her arrival. She waits. Eventually she hears the front door open, slam shut and a man's voice shouting, "Mor, I'm back!" She assumes this is William Hunter at last. Another silence. She envisages Alice Mor hurrying down to the hallway, finger to her lips, to intercept the man and inform him of her presence.

At length, booted footsteps clatter down the stairs and the kitchen door is thrust open. A tall dandyish man with an elaborately waxed moustache, side whispers and a mane of red gold curls enters the kitchen, filling it with his presence. He wears cord trousers, a tweed jacket and a floppy yellow paisley cravat.

"Aha. You are Box 21, I presume," he booms.

Lucy agrees.

Walter Hunter leans his hands on the table. He studies her face intently, his leonine head on one side, as if he were considering whether she might be a suitable subject for a painting. Refusing to be intimidated, she stares back. This is her best and so far, her only lead. She must pursue it; however uncomfortable it is making her feel.

"Yes," he says finally. "I see." He walks over to the dresser and helps himself to a biscuit from a tin with a picture of Queen Victoria's coronation on the side. He does not offer her one.

"You seek information on the whereabouts of a young girl and a boy?"

Lucy agrees this is her mission. "I am led to believe from Mrs Mor that you know them. She told me their names. I deliberately did not name them in the advertisement."

Hunter rolls his eyes. "Yes. Dear Alice. A good maker but not a very discreet individual. Now, Miss …?"

"Landseer."

"Indeed. Let us lay our cards on the table. I encountered the two children while seeking inspiration for a work of art. They posed for me. Subsequently, they sojourned here for a short time, acting as my models. The boy is not much to look at, but the girl ~ ah, the girl is a wonder!"

"Are they still here?"

He shakes his head. "They departed very early one morning while we were all still abed. No word of farewell or divulging of destination. Looking back, we recalled talking about a police matter ~ nothing to do with us, I hasten to add. We think they went as a result of overhearing that conversation, suggesting that they may have committed some criminal act and were afraid of being apprehended."

"No, you are quite wrong," Lucy says firmly. "Clearly, they did not take you into their confidence. So, allow me to lay out the facts behind my investigation." And she proceeds to tell Hunter the story of Sam Thomas, his family, and the escape from the Union Workhouse. "I am tasked with finding Mr. Thomas' two children and returning them to his care. So, do you have any idea where they may have gone?"

Walter Hunter shakes his head, spreads his hands in a dramatic gesture. "Alas, I do not."

Lucy tries to keep her voice level. "Then I do not quite see why you contacted me, and how you can help my investigation."

Hunter produces a paintbrush from an outer pocket and taps his cheek with it. "It is not so much how I can help you, as how you can help me," he says loftily. "I must have the girl to sit for me again. She is my muse. I hoped, as a result of coming forward with the information I have provided, that I would be able to avail myself of her when you eventually find her. Your advertisement mentioned a reward. This is the only reward I seek."

Lucy is lost for words. The sheer brazen selfishness of the man! Summoning up every ounce of self-control she possesses, she rises from her seat, holding on to the edge of the table to stop herself from boxing his ears. "In that case, Mr. Hunter, I bid you good day," she says coldly. "And let me assure you, if I find Fletcher and Eliza Thomas, I shall be dispatching them on the next ship for New York at once. Their poor father has not seen his beloved children for many years. He was not able even to furnish me with an accurate description of them." There are two spots of anger in her cheeks as she finishes, and her voice trembles with anger.

Disconcerted, Hunter looks off. "Oh, I see. Ah. Well, as to that, Miss … Landseer, I may be able to help you after all. I have a folder of sketches and watercolours that I made when the two children were here. If you will permit me, I shall fetch it down and you can take a look."

Hunter goes. When he returns, he is accompanied by Alice Mor, a dark-haired man with a hammer and a bandage on one hand, and a black artists' portfolio. He places the portfolio on the kitchen table and unties the ribbon. "Here are some charcoal sketches, a few pen and ink drawings and a couple of watercolours."

Lucy sifts through the artwork. However much she has taken an instant dislike to Walter Hunter (and she has), she has to admit that his work is very fine. She picks up a watercolour painting. It shows the two children standing by an open window, framed by a striped curtain. Flitch is looking at his sister; Eliza holds a bowl of purple crocuses.

"Do you like it?" Hunter says. Mutely, she nods. Lucy is so engaged by the picture that she does not notice the nods and significant glances being exchanged between the three artists. She places the it back on the table. "Thank you for showing me these," she says, re-tying her bonnet strings.

There is a pause. Then Hunter coughs, clears his throat. "I, that is to say, we would like to present you with the watercolour. Mrs Mor suggests that it could be sent to the father in New York. We are sorry we cannot help you in your search, but perhaps this might give him pleasure?"

Lucy's face brightens instantly. "Thank you; I think it would indeed," she exclaims.

Alice Mor rolls up the painting and secures it with string. "Of course, if they ever come back to us, we will send for you immediately," she says quietly, touching Lucy's sleeve as she goes over to the door leading up to the street and opens it for her.

****

So what has happened to Eliza, the 'wonder girl'? We left her frozen with shock, watching her brother being dragged off by the workhouse overseer. "Run!" Flitch commanded her. But Liza has absolutely no intention of running anywhere. Quickly pulling herself together, she stealthily creeps after them, inching into doorways and alleys whenever it seems she might be spotted. She watches from behind an upturned boat as Flitch is manhandled into The Ships Arms and the door is slammed and bolted behind him.

Time passes. Liza stays in position, keeping watch. She sees the landlord affixing a notice to the door of the public house. She sees candles being lit on the ground floor. She ventures forth and approaches the door. The notice says CLOSED. She lays her head against the rough wood, listening. Nothing. She retreats to her hiding place and resumes her solitary watch. Candles are lit at an upstairs window, making pools of warm yellow light amidst the shadows. She sees outlines of people pass and repass. They are not Flitch.

Eventually, Liza gives in to her weariness. They are not going to do anything to her brother tonight. She needs to get her head down for a few hours before returning tomorrow. Stifling her sobs, she makes her way back to the cheap lodging house and climbs the stairs to the tiny room she and her brother are renting.

Liza curls up on the bare mattress, watching the stars in the night sky and waiting for sleep to come. She has no money to pay for another night, nor to buy herself breakfast tomorrow morning. She will have to sell some of their meagre possessions to keep going. But keep going she will. Until she can be with her brother once more. At least one of them is free. Now that free one must do all they can to release the other.

Liza could have sworn that she didn't sleep a wink all night, but the next thing she knows is sunlight streaming in at the dirty uncurtained window and the sound of two lodgers having a heated argument on the landing outside. She pushes herself to a stand, rubbing the grit out of her eyes. Then she collects up the two bundles, that have been carefully stowed away under a cracked washstand and makes her way downstairs, carefully avoiding the two quarrelsome men.

Mrs O'Malley, the owner of the lodging house (*Clane beds. Mangling done*) is in the basement kitchen, preparing breakfast for those who have paid for it. Liza's mouth waters as the fragrant smells of frying bacon come wafting enticingly up the stairs. She peeks into the small breakfast parlour, currently unoccupied. The table is set for four. A rack of toast is growing cold and leathery on a sideboard. She darts in, snaffles a couple of slices and makes her escape through the front door.

Liza heads back to The Ships Head. She isn't sure exactly what she can do to free her brother, she just knows she needs to be where he is. When she reaches the public house however, she is surprised to find the front door wide open, and a small crowd gathered outside. They are being addressed by the big bull of a man she remembers as the owner. Liza pulls her bonnet down over her forehead and wraps her shawl around her lower face.

"Escaped from under our very noses," the landlord's voice booms. "A desperate young criminal wot stole the fam'ly jewels from my poor sufferin' sister. She took him in out of the goodness of her hart when he was an orfling and this is how she is repaid!"

The crowd murmurs its collective disgust.

"We had the boy locked up in the attic, all ready for the police to apprehend and charge, but the blighter escaped overnight."

"How'd he do it?" a voice in the crowd asks, interestedly.

"Shinned up the bleedin' chimbley, would you believe? Then got out onto the roof and he was away. My pore sister is sittin' in the parlour, the tears a-running down her cheeks. Her man is scouring the area with a couple of policemen. He won't have gone far though, and we are going to make sure he goes no farther than a prison cell."

"Quite right too," a woman declares stoutly. "There's far too much of this pilfering going on. I blame the parents. They let them run wild on the street, picking up all sorts of bad ways and getting into trouble. Saucing their elders and betters too. I've heard them. In my day,

146

you wasn't allowed out of your backyard until you was old enough to go to work."

Liza has heard enough. She slips away, ducking down an alleyway. Once she feels confident she is far enough away from the public house not to be of any interest, she squats down and opens the bundles. She needs to sort out what are essential to survive, and what she can do without. It's only temporary, she reminds herself, as she redistributes the contents into two piles. Once she is reunited with Flitch, they will buy back everything, she promises herself.

Having sorted her worldly goods and chattels, Liza sets off to find somewhere to turn half of them into cash. She walks until she reaches a row of shops running parallel to a large warehouse. She passes an undertaker, an apothecary, a greengrocer whose vegetables all have a damp and scaly appearance, as if they had been crossed with fish and seaweed.

Finally, Liza passes a marine store with a small, black-faced doll hanging in the window. From the odd spoons, single chipped plates, handkerchiefs, soiled pairs of boots, pewter watches and tobacco pipes that constitute the window display, she is pretty sure she has reached her destination. She enters, marches up to the counter and hoists up one of the bundles. It contains the fur rug, a pretty fringed shawl, and several lengths of bright ribbon.

"How much for these things?" she asks the man behind the counter, who tuts as he starts examining them.

"They yours to sell?" he says, glaring at her.

She nods. "So, how much will you give me?"

He rolls his eyes, names a sum. It is less than she wants, but sufficient for her current needs. The man gives her a 'don't even think about bargaining' look. Reluctantly, she agrees to his proposal. He sweeps her possessions off the counter, writes her out a ticket, then opens his cashbox and counts out the coins.

Liza pockets them, picks up the other bundle and leaves the dolly shop. Flitch won't be happy about the fur rug, she thinks ruefully, as she walks away from the docks. But now she has some money, she can get herself a proper meal and then the search for her brother can begin. It never occurs to Liza that they won't be reunited. After all the years they spent apart, in the workhouse, that is not a thought she is prepared to entertain. Sooner or later, their paths will cross, and they will be together once more.

****

Actually, unbeknown to both Liza and Flitch, their paths have already crossed. After spending a few hours huddled in a doorway, waiting for first light, Flitch makes his way back to the lodging house to see if his sister has returned and is waiting for him. Slipping in through the unlocked front door, he tiptoes up to the second floor and opens the door. The room is empty. Liza and their bundles have gone.

Flitch crosses the room, then squats down in front of the washstand. He eases up a floorboard, and retrieves a small bag, which chinks as he transfers it to an inner pocket. Then he closes the door quietly and goes back out into the busy street.

A short while later, Flitch is heading towards the West India Docks, his eyes peeled for a small, shawled figure carrying two bundles. He knows that despite his command to run, Liza won't have obeyed him. She will be here, somewhere in the tangle of narrow streets and twisting alleyways, waiting for him to find her. All he has to do is avoid the Union overseer, his wife, the landlord of The Ships Head and his wife, their friends and the police!

****

Meanwhile Detective Constable Tom Williams is doggedly pursuing his own line of inquiries. His first stop is the premises of Jarvis & Co., land speculators and pullers down of ancient houses. They are the main rivals of Barrowclough and Cuthbert, and as he has recently learned from Richard Cuthbert, James Barrowclough used to work for the company when he first arrived in London.

There is clearly a story here, and Williams is determined to extract it, which is why he is currently standing in the atrium of the building, awaiting the arrival of Mr. Dan Jarvis, with whom he has secured a meeting. After sufficient time has elapsed, Tom is shown into the inner sanctum of the owner of the business.

Tom Williams is used to the uproar and confusion of the officers' day room, where his colleagues write their reports, snatch a few minutes sleep, eat hurried meals and spill tea on the desk. He is used to Mr. Stride's office, to which the words municipal dustheap could be applied. The office of Mr. Jarvis is another world altogether.

There is a desk ~ which is so large it takes up almost the entire width of the room. There is a gold-backed chair behind the desk. Two comfortable armchairs. A portrait of a former Mr. Jarvis in a high wing collar and dark suit that was probably fashionable many years ago. There are ornate rugs on the highly polished floor. Framed maps of the English counties adorn every wall. The room smells of polish and a rather unpleasant hair pomade.

"Now then, officer," says the current Mr. Jarvis, a sly foxy-faced man with well-oiled hair and moustache, after he has settled Tom in one of the armchairs and sent out for coffee, "to what do I owe this unexpected visit? I assure you whatever wind blows you to my neck of the jungle, I can account for my movements, and I probably have at least three witnesses who will back me up." He pauses. "That was a joke."

"Ah, I see, sir," Williams says, his features deadpan. "Actually, I am not here to accuse you of any crime. I would like you to tell me how you met the late Mr. James Barrowclough, whom I gather used to work for your business before he set up with his partner."

Jarvis looks puzzled. "Ain't he dead and buried?"

"Indeed. But Scotland Yard is still interested in the cause of his demise."

"Fell under a train, as I read it in the newspapers."

"That was certainly a contributory factor," Williams agrees. He gets out his notebook. "So, can you remember the first time you met Mr. Barrowclough, sir?"

Jarvis frowns, stares at the far corner of the room. Pulls at his moustache. Taps his fingers on the desk. "Oh, I remember it very well, officer. Ought not to speak ill of the dead, but not the sort of thing you forget in a hurry. Got a nice sharp pencil there, have you? Right, where shall I begin?"

By the time Tom Williams leaves, he has a very clear picture of the young James William Malin Barrowclough, a man in a tearing hurry, who arrived in London from his home town of Birmingham determined to make both a name and a fortune for himself as quickly as possible, and escape the stifling and restricting world of his strict factory-owning Methodist father.

Barrowclough had arrived with a pocketbook stuffed full of banknotes ("Between you, me and the gatepost, I suspected that he raided the office safe before he flitted," Jarvis said), and within a week, he had engaged a smart set of rooms off Bond Street, bought some smart suits and shrugged off his northern industrial origins.

The only thing that still marked him out was his northern accent, but even that was dealt with courtesy of lessons from a good elocution tutor, and by the end of three months, you might have met the young Barrowclough at any middle-class party or soirée and never known he was anything but a well-dressed, well spoken, affluent man about town.

Jarvis met him at the racetrack, shortly after he'd arrived in London. They struck up a conversation and got on really well, to begin with. Barrowclough seemed like the sort of keen young man he was looking for to train up in the ruthless cutthroat world of the land speculator and developer. So he took him on as a junior partner, introduced him to his Club, taught him the business. And for several years, they rubbed along pretty amicably.

But then Barrowclough decided that he needed to move a few rungs further up the social ladder. So he started courting a Miss Helena Chapman, only daughter of a top QC and his upper-class wife. The family owned a fine Hampstead house and moved amongst the sort of social circles that a parvenu from the midlands could only view from afar. But amazingly, he was accepted into their milieu.

Jarvis, who watched all this happen, gave it as his opinion that Miss Helena, who was in her late twenties and as pallid and insipid as warm milk, had been on the shelf for years, so when the chance came to marry her off, the family weren't going to inquire too deeply into the background of the young man with impeccable manners and sharp tailoring who turned up at their gate, handsome princes on white steeds being in short supply over the age of eighteen.

Marriage, followed by two boys, followed by the deaths in quick succession of the elderly QC and his spouse only increased Barrowclough's luck. He started angling for a full partnership, which Jarvis was reluctant to agree to. By this time, he just didn't like the man, he told Williams. Didn't like the way he dealt with people. Didn't like his flashes of temper when he was thwarted over a matter. Luckily, the refusal coincided with the appearance on the scene of Richard Cuthbert ~ or Dicky Cutthroat as Jarvis called him. In Cuthbert, Barrowclough met his equal: a man as unscrupulous and egotistical as he was.

And so, Barrowclough and Cuthbert set up in business together, the one using the skills he'd learned from Jarvis and the capital accrued from selling his dead father's house and later, the factory, the other using his acumen for sniffing out a good deal and pouncing on it. And they prospered. They undercut other companies. They poached their prospective clients. They sent out spies to make sure they were the first to secure land. They became rich and hated in the dog-eat-dog world of developers and land speculators. (Which said a lot, Williams thought.)

Detective Constable Tom Williams has a lot to think about as he makes his way back to Scotland Yard. What he is mainly thinking about is that the origins of everything that happened to Barrowclough clearly went back further than his arrival in London. So he, therefore, must also travel further back into the dead man's past to solve the mystery of his death.

****

We left Flitch in possession of a bag of coins, earned from his skill at cards, but with no idea where his sister might be. He decides to search the area, scanning every shop doorway, every alley and passageway he passes. For the first time since their arrival, he is overwhelmed by the vastness of the place. How can he possibly find Liza amidst the noise and din, the hustle and bustle of the busy streets, where everybody rushes past him with a purposeful expression, not realising that he has lost the most precious thing in his life, and not caring to give him the time of day.

Clammy fingers of memory reach out for his heart. Why does the present feel so much like a reworking of the past? Meanwhile, his feet continue taking him towards the West India Docks. Eventually they reach the Limehouse causeway and stop outside a building with an inscription in Chinese characters over the lintel. There are delicious smells of cooking emerging from the open door. Flitch sniffs the air. He is starving. Next minute, his feet are mounting the steps and taking him inside in search of something tasty to eat.

Flitch doesn't know it, but the inscription informs passers-by that this is the Chinese Mission House, run for sailors and merchants off the ships who want a temporary and safe lodging place in between voyages. He stands in the foyer waiting for somebody to appear and tell him to go away. When they fail to materialise, he follows his nose and finds himself in a large kitchen. There are a couple of cooks in small hats and long aprons. The contents of huge round pots are being tossed and shaken over naked flames. Bowls and plates are being counted and stacked. Heated discussions in a language alien to his ear are taking place. Flitch stands on the threshold, his gaze going from one person to another until someone notices him.

"A boy!" a man says, pointing directly at him.

There is a murmur of agreement.

"You hungry, boy?" the man asks. Flitch nods mutely. The man scoops a ladleful of food from a pot, pours it into a porcelain bowl decorated with red dragons and beckons him over. "Boy, sit here and eat," he says, placing the bowl and two slender sticks on the table. Flitch obeys. He picks up the two sticks, holds them together and attempts to lever a small piece of cooked vegetable onto them. There is a chorus of laughter. He is handed a spoon and soon the contents of the bowl have vanished. A cup with no handles is placed before him. It is full of a pale liquid that emits curls of steam. He blows on the surface until it is cool, then drinks it down.

"I know this boy," says his benefactor. "This is 'Find the Lady' boy. Very clever. Very good at getting money from poor hard-up Chinese sailors, eh?" he continues. Flitch regards him cautiously, but there is a smile in his eyes as he speaks. Flitch grins back.

"Thanks for the food," he says, getting up and carrying his bowl over to a sink. The man waves him back to his seat. He ladles some food into another bowl and takes it to the table, seating himself opposite Flitch. Removing a pair of chopsticks from a pocket, he holds the bowl close to his face and proceeds to transfer the contents from bowl to mouth. Flitch watches, fascinated. When the man has emptied the bowl, he picks up the conversation again.

"So, what're you doing in Limehouse, 'Find the Lady' boy? You're not from round here. I know most people from round here. And where is the girl?"

Suddenly, Flitch feels a pain in the place where tears come from. He brushes his eyes with his coat sleeve. "I don't know," he gulps, turning his head away. "She got lost somewhere."

Silence falls. The only sound comes from the bubbling pots and the hiss of the gas. Flitch leans his arms on the table and buries his face. His shoulders shake. Dimly, he is aware that the man has risen from his seat and come round to his side of the table. An arm is put round his shoulders. "My young friend, you've come to the right place. I am Pastor Chang, and this is the Chinese Mission House. If you have any trouble, we will help you."

Flitch lifts a tear-streaked face. "Why? I ain't Chinese."

"My wife is English," Pastor Chang tells him. "We help any people who cross our threshold. It is what we are here to do. Now, 'Find the Lady' boy, we are about to serve lunch to our guests. You stay here, in the warm. After, we will talk and see what can be done."

He issues a string of commands to the kitchen staff, who pick up piles of plates, bowls and chopsticks and head out of the kitchen, followed by the cooks carrying the huge pots. Left on his own, Flitch is suddenly overcome by weariness. He rests his head on his arms and lets himself drift away into darkness.

Flitch wakes to the sound of voices in the background. For a moment, terror seizes him: he imagines that he is back in the public house, with the leering faces of the overseer and his wife taunting him with what they intend to do. He starts up with a cry, which instantly dies away when he realises that the voices come from a group of dark-haired, black-eyed youngsters, watching him from the far side of the room.

A boy, same age as Flitch, slightly built, in a blue padded jacket and nankeen trousers steps forward. "I am Li Wei," he says. "My father runs this mission house. This is my sister Rose, her friend Tillie, and my useless little brother Berthold."

"I am NOT useless," the small boy says indignantly. He looks to be about four years old.

"We do not yet know your name," Li Wei says, politely, "but my father tells us you have lost your friend. We wish to help you find her."

Flitch tells them his name. "She's my sister Liza," he says. "We were visiting the docks, and I got taken … look, it's a long story. Maybe I should just go. Easier all round, eh?"

Li Wei regards him steadily. "Maybe. Or maybe you should stay. We have all the time in the world to listen to stories. Why not come to my room. We won't be disturbed by anybody. You can tell us your story, and we will work out a plan to find your sister. What do you say?"

Flitch shrugs. "Nuffink to lose, I suppose. Though I don't see how you can help."

The girl called Rose smiles, showing small white pointed teeth. "We are small, you see. So we can go wherever we like. All places. Nobody notices us, because we are only children, and we are Chinese, so they think we do not matter. We can listen at keyholes and spy through windows. If your sister is staying anywhere round here, one of us will find her and bring her back to you."

Her words make sense. Flitch remembers how rumours and stories spread through the Union Workhouse via the younger inmates. It was how he found out about Ma's death; how he communicated with Liza; how he knew about the loose bar on the window; how they coordinated their escape. So he follows them as they trek across an unpainted dining hall, through a low door at the far end, and up some twisty stairs until they reach a tiny room with a bed, a hanging cupboard, a small oak desk and chair, and a view over the river.

Li Wei closes the door. Rose sets her back to it. Tillie and Berthold sit on the bare floorboards. Flitch hovers by the window.

"And now," the boy says, sitting on the chair and turning to face him, "we are entirely alone. We cannot be overheard." He nods at Flitch in a friendly fashion. "Please, tell us your story."

So Flitch tells them. From the beginning, from the time when they were a family to his imprisonment in the attic of The Ships Head. It takes some time, and the light is fading gently in the western sky by the time he is done. The group listen in silence, occasionally nodding or tutting in sympathy. When he has talked himself to a standstill, Li Wei gets up and goes over to stand next to him. He puts an arm round Flitch's shoulder.

"You are no longer alone, Flitch. Nor is Liza. I will ask my father if you can stay in one of our guest rooms tonight. Tomorrow, we start the search. We have friends all over Limehouse ~ they will join us. Now, we will go and get our supper and then we shall all go to bed. We must make an early start tomorrow: if the police are after you and your sister, there is no time to lose."

****

The overseer of the Union Workhouse and his partner in crime would certainly agree with Li Wei's sentiment that there is no time to lose. Here they are in the back parlour of The Ships Head, together with mine host and hostess, considering their options. The escape of Flitch Thomas has put them temporarily on the back foot, but there are always other feet.

"I bin thinking," says the landlord, stroking his chin, which at this time of the morning is blue and unshaven. "You say this lady detective doesn't know what them two tykes looks like."

"Only what we told her," says the overseer's wife, pouting.

"Right. Right. So, if you turned up on her doorstep with a boy and a girl who looked like them two … similar heights and ages, kind of thing, she might believe you found them?"

"And hand over the reward!" the overseer says, his face brightening at the thought.

"But where'd we find two kids like that?" His wife frowns.

The landlord looks sly. He taps the side of his nose with an index finger. "We 'make' them. I know plenty of customers who have children the same ages. We just dress them up and tell them exactly what to say. Easy."

"And the reward?" The overseer can see where this might be going.

"Well, obviously you'd have to offer something. Can't expect to borrow people's kids for nothing. But it'd be better than no reward at all, wouldn't it?"

There is a pause while the overseer and his wife turn this new suggestion over and around, looking for holes.

"We'd have to rescue them before they got sent to America."

"The sort of kids I have in mind wouldn't need rescuing; they'd escape. Remember, she ain't exactly going to keep them under lock and key, is she? Two kids off to see their long-lost father. If they want to go for a little walk before they board the big ship, she won't say no, will she?"

The overseer nods, grudgingly. "Sounds like you got it all worked out."

"So, are you in?"

"We're in."

The landlord grins. "I got a couple of kids in mind already. Should have them here by mid-morning, all ready for you to turn them into a Flitch and Liza their own mother wouldn't recognise."

And true to his word, a few hours later, the landlord returns to The Ships Head accompanied by a boy and a girl whom he introduces as Lily and Arthur Klem.

"They know what they have to do," he says, as the overseer and his wife walk round the two fake Thomases, examining them closely. "Just give them a few personal bits and pieces to sound convincing."

"The girl's hair is too dark," the overseer's wife says. "And too long."

"We'll cut it, flour it and clap a bonnet on her. Anything else?"

She shakes her head. "You done a good job finding them, Bill, I must say."

The landlord preens. "You got the address of the lady detective?"

She produces a business card. "I have it here. Her address is Baker Street."

"Then you write to her. Do it now, is my advice. Say you found the kids and when should you bring them round. Soon as you get a reply, we'll do the business and make them up to look like the ones she wants. Then you take them to her, collect the reward, and by the time she's realised they ain't the kids she thinks they are, you'll be back in Cambridge, and we'll all be a lot richer."

The overseer regards the landlord approvingly. "It's perfect, ain't it. She won't know any different. And we get our hands on all that money."

"Some of the money," the landlord reminds him.

"Oh, yeah, that was what I meant, o'course," the overseer adds hastily. "C'mon my dear, let me help you write that letter. We don't want to make any mistakes, do we?"

The two lookalikes are dismissed but told to remain on standby awaiting further instructions. Meanwhile, the overseer and his wife mount the stairs to the first floor.

"So, what do I write?" his wife asks, as she sucks the end of a quill.

"Just what he said," her husband replies. "We found Flitch and Liza; they can't wait to be reunited with their father. When shall we deliver them?"

The overseer's wife scribbles a few lines, making several blots.

"There's just one thing," the overseer says, lowering his voice. "Once we leave here with those two kids, we won't be coming back, so make sure you take all your things with you. Not too obvious like."

Her eyes snap open in surprise. "We ain't coming back? Why not?"

He pulls a face. "You think I'm going to share that money? Listen to me, as soon as we've got shot of the kids and been paid, we're on the first train out of London. Your sister and her man can whistle for their share. Now, you write that letter and I'll give it to the postman when he calls."

****

So what has happened to Eliza Thomas, whom we left pawning some of her worldly goods to survive? After leaving the dolly shop, she walks around the area, looking for her brother, until hunger drives her into a small baker and confectioner's, where she buys a stale loaf and a small cake, which she takes down to the dockside and eats while sitting on a convenient bollard. Seagulls swoop above her, screaming their indignation that she isn't sharing her provender.

Liza finishes her food, shakes out her dress and continues her search. It is beginning to dawn on her that the Docks extend far further than The Ships Head, the surrounding streets and Mrs O'Malley's lodging house. If she wishes to stay in the area until she and her brother are reunited, she must source a place to lay her head. And some means of supplementing her meagre supply of money. Liza has her pride; she refuses to beg. So she will have to seek out some other employment.

Thinking out how to accomplish this, she finds herself walking down Dock Street, where a handsome and spacious house, set a little apart from the rest, brings her to a sudden halt. There is a woman in an apron with a bucket of soapy water down on her knees scrubbing the front steps. Liza approaches her cautiously.

"Good day, Miss," she says in her best and most polite voice, "My name is Eliza. I am from the workhouse, and I am looking for work. I can wash, scrub, sew, and make bread. Do you have a vacancy for someone who can do all these things?"

The woman sits back on her heels and surveys her slowly from top to toe. Liza tries to project incredible willingness. "How old are you?" the woman asks finally.

"Eleven."

"Bit small, ain't you?"

"They didn't feed us much."

The woman puffs out her breath. "Well, I don't know. I could do with a helping hand, that's for sure. But how do I know you won't run away."

Liza mirrors indignation. "I am not that sort of girl. Please let me work for you. I promise I won't let you down."

There is a pause. Liza holds her breath. Then the woman levers herself to her feet. "Well, these steps won't clean themselves and I have better things to do with my time. Let's see how you get on," she says grudgingly, handing her the vicious looking scrubbing brush. "Make a good job of it and I might take you on."

Liza sets down her bundle and picks up the scrubbing brush. It has been some time since she handled one, but she finds that the knack hasn't left her. In no time at all, the step is white and sparkling and …well, perhaps she wouldn't want to eat her dinner off it. But she wouldn't mind some dinner. She empties the bucket into the street, collects her bundle and treks inside.

Her work is inspected and given a seal of approval. A piece of bread and a heel of cheese is handed over with instructions to eat it on the back step and then start the washing up. As she munches her food, Liza reviews her situation. While scrubbing the step, she'd noticed a plaque on the wall: *Sailors' Rest: Superior Rooms for Mariners. Prop. C. Dixon.* From the harassed staff, she gathers that Mrs Caroline Dixon is a middle-aged widow, who opened the *Sailors' Rest* a few years ago upon the demise of her ship's captain husband from yellow fever on a voyage to Madagascar.

The *Sailors' Rest* caters for captains and officers. Mrs Dixon is very particular about her clientele. Oh yes. None of the below decks' riffraff, and strictly no foreigners either. This is no hole and corner boarding house. "She will work you into the ground," Liza is warned. "Meggie, who did the scrubbing and washing before you turned up, walked out yesterday. Said she'd rather take her chances on the streets. That's why Mrs D. was scrubbing the step herself, coz none of us do outside work. I'd leave now if I were you."

But Liza can't leave; she has no option but to stay. She and Flitch are being sought by the overseer and his wife, who want to return them to a life of drudgery and beatings. The police are also involved in the search. A roof over her head, food and the chance of finding her brother some day is enough to convince her. Besides, however hard the work, it surely can't be any harder than life in the Union Workhouse, could it?

****

The railway system of England and Scotland is one of the wonders of the Victorian age. The line from London to Birmingham Curzon Street was opened in the 1830s and by 1839 had carried 267,527 passengers from Babylondon to Birmingham and back. Originally, the carriages were open at the sides and third class was unroofed. Now, in the late 1860s, things have improved immeasurably. Carriages have roofs, and sides. They are still unheated, although first class passengers are provided with foot warmers and cushions depending upon the season. There are no corridors though, and no lavatories. And should anything untoward occur, there is no way of contacting a guard.

Not that any of this perturbs Detective Constable Tom Williams, who has never in his whole life ventured outside the city of London. He was born here, received his education here, joined a London police office as a beat constable, and has been working the mean streets and the meaner paperwork ever since. Thus it is with a sense of both excitement and slight apprehension that he alights from an omnibus and enters the huge hall of Euston Square Station. Making his way across to the booking office he purchases his train ticket to Birmingham New Street.

Earlier in the week, Williams wrote to the Birmingham town police to alert them to his arrival and outline the reasons why he is making the long journey up north. He has solicited their help in tracking down any information about the Barrowclough family. He hopes this will shorten his time in what, to him, is terra incognita.

His ticket bought, Tom makes his way to the platform, where at the far end, the green L&NWR locomotive is being coaled and watered ready for its journey. On the advice of a colleague, he has purchased a second-class ticket, ("You don't ever want to travel third-class, mate. Just take my word for it."). Now he walks along the platform and boards the train, selecting a seat facing the engine and next to the window. He has also been advised not to do this, as the chances of soot and cinders in the eyes and smoke in the lungs are high, but sometimes, especially if you are a young person, you make your own decisions in life.

Tom Williams settles himself comfortably on the bench seat. He has a long journey ahead of him, so he has brought his Police Manual with him to study, as well as his notes on the Barrowclough investigation. He also has a packet of sandwiches, a bottle of beer and complete faith that his bladder will last the journey.

The carriage fills up. A respectable looking couple take their places in the opposite corner. An elderly clergyman sits opposite them. Then, with a shout from the guard, a wave of a green flag and a shriek from the engine, the train slowly pulls out of the station and chugs away, gathering speed as it progresses through the north London suburbs with their huddled tenements and row upon row of newly-built brick houses.

Gradually, as the urban landscape gives way to fields, woods and small hamlets, Tom succumbs to the soothing rhythm of iron wheels on iron rails. The respectable couple talk in low tones about various domestic issues. The clergyman studies and annotates his bible. Tom attempts to get to grips with the finer points of legal procedures in the apprehension of street felons, but the words start to swim on the page, then his eyes close and his head lolls and before long, he is fast asleep.

A brief stop at Rugby clears the carriage of three of its occupants and replaces them with a harassed young mother with a fractious baby and two small children. Tom, who is fond of children, attempts to entertain them by making a puppet from his pocket handkerchief ~

something his own father used to do. After regarding him with some trepidation, the two children gradually relinquish their shyness and the three spend the journey from Rugby to Birmingham sharing an exciting story about brave knight Sir Handkin, a fiery dragon and a fair princess who requires constant rescuing. Such is his success that as the train reaches the ribbon development surrounding the town, the children plead with their mother to let them take Tom home with them.

At last, the train pulls into New Street Station and comes to a steaming halt at the buffers. Detective Constable Williams collects his belongings, helps his fellow passengers down to the platform, bids the two children farewell and strides off towards the barrier. He leaves the station, noting that the advertisements for Bovril, HP sauce and Birds custard, on the walls leading to the street are exactly the same as the ones in London. There, however, the similarity ends.

From the moment Williams steps out into the thronged thoroughfare, his ears are assailed by the hammering of presses and the clatter of engines. The noise of Birmingham is beyond description. He makes his way along streets bustling with workers returning home from their shift, their faces coated with dust and oil, and those clocking on for the night shift going in the opposite direction.

There are dust heaps everywhere. The streets do not ever appear to have been sluiced. Tom steps over piles of litter, and manure, oily black water, bones, rotten vegetables. Flies buzz, stray dogs fight. Great carts loaded with coal, lime and iron bars queue from one street to another, their drivers shouting at each other in an accent he does not understand. By the time he reaches the small hotel where a room has been booked for him, Tom Williams' ears are ringing from the din, and he feels as if his throat wants sweeping, like some domestic chimney.

Williams gives his name to the porter and receives a key on a piece of string and the information that "Breakfast is served from 7.30 till 8.30, not a minute before nor a minute after." He is just about to carry his bag up the stairs to the second-floor room, when the man calls him back. He has a letter in his hand. "Came this afternoon," he says laconically.

Williams tucks the letter into his coat pocket. Later, when he has unpacked, settled in, written the first of his reports for Inspector Greig, and is preparing to go out in search of a late supper (not served at the hotel), he decides to address himself to the letter. Sitting on the creaky bed with its thin mattress, he opens it. The missive comes from a Mr. George Glossop, Chief Constable. After the usual polite greetings from one colleague to another (he clearly is unaware of Tom's lowly status in the police hierarchy), Glossop writes that he will be available to discuss the matter in hand tomorrow at his police office at 9.30. Certain inquiries have been made as a result of Detective Williams' initial communication and he is now in a position to share some findings with his esteemed colleague. Yours etc etc.

It is with a hopeful heart, therefore, and high expectations that Tom sallies forth to find a hostelry. Having eaten a plate of thickly sliced beef in some curious gravy and drunk a pint of rather strong ale, he beds down for the night to the accompaniment of hammering and clanging as the huge factory machines beat out their relentless rhythm in the darkness.

****

It is a bright clear morning, and at The Ships Head, work has begun early to transform Lily and Arthur Klem into

Eliza and Flitch Thomas. Alongside various tweaks and alterations, both children are being schooled into what they must say, and how they should answer any questions put to them.

"You remember what you have to do?" the overseer asks.

The children look puzzled.

"Nothing. You do nothing; you say nothing. Just agree that you are Eliza and Flitch Thomas. Leave everything else up to me and the wife. I'll answer any questions. You stay stumm. Just try to look like you're thrilled to be going to see your pa after all these years."

The girl, Lily Klem, pulls a face. "So when do we get the reward? Coz you promised us a reward, didn't yer?"

The overseer and his wife exchange a quick and meaningful look over the top of her head. "You get the reward when you've done exactly what we told you. Got it? Now, are we all set? I told the detective lady we'd be there by dinnertime."

They prepare to leave. The overseer's wife has tied her bags around her waist and covered them with her cloak. They pause in the bar for the children to be scrutinised and admired.

"We're off now," the overseer says, pushing the youngsters towards the door. "See you soon."

As the little party exits into the street, they almost trip over a small black-haired child, who is playing in the dirt outside. The landlord kicks him roughly aside. "Get out of the way! Bloody Chinks. They're everywhere. Like yellow rats they are. Be off with you!"

The overseer, his wife and the lookalike Flitch and Eliza head for the omnibus stop. Meanwhile, Berthold brushes himself down, and speeds off to inform the others what he has overheard and just witnessed.

A few hours later, after a brief pitstop for refreshments and a bit of spit and polishing of the candidates, the overseer and his wife arrive outside 122A Baker Street and after ringing the bell, are let into the hallway by the small maid of all work.

"Now, you just remember what I told you," the overseer hisses over his shoulder, as the four climb the stairs to the first floor, and halt outside a door bearing the plaque: L. Landseer, Private Detective. He raps on the door, which is opened by a smiling Lucy Landseer. The smile, however, begins to lose itself rapidly at the edges as she glances down at the two fake Thomases.

"Now then, Miss ... Landseer," the overseer says, seemingly unperturbed by Lucy's change of facial expression. "Here they are. Flitch and Liza Thomas. All neat and tidy and ready to set off to America to meet their Pa. Can't wait to set sail. I told you we'd find them, didn't I?"

"Oh, indeed you did," Lucy murmurs, standing aside so that the four can enter her office. She places the overseer's wife in the clientele chair and indicates that the two children should approach her desk for inspection. The overseer positions himself by the door, arms folded, a smug grin on his porcine features.

"So, you are Fletcher, and you are Eliza?" Lucy says, addressing the two youngsters.

"They are indeed," the overseer's wife breaks in. "And a mort of trouble they've caused us. We had to come all the way down from Cambridge to find them. But, after what you told us, miss, we decided that nothing was too much trouble. And so, here they are."

Lucy barely glances in her direction. "Well, Fletcher and Eliza," she says, evenly, "what have you been up to since you escaped from the Union Workhouse? For I shall have to write to your father and inform him that you are found, and you are coming to be with him, and he will want to know."

The girl who isn't Eliza casts a desperate glance over to the door.

"They don't remember much of it," the overseer says. "London being such a big place and all that. But they can't wait to be with their lovin' Pa again, ain't that right?"

Both youngsters nod vigorously, this being a part of the script that they are familiar with.

"I see," Lucy says. "Yes indeed, I see clearly. So, Fletcher and Eliza Thomas, I am delighted to meet you at last. Now, you must be aware that in the search to find you, I have been offered many boys and girls who turned out to be fake. So many, that I am considering reporting them and those who presented them to me to the Metropolitan Police. Forgery is a crime, you know and pretending to be somebody you aren't, is a crime also." She pauses, pretends to consult a folder on her desk, but watches the occupants of the room from under lowered eyelids. Panicky glances are exchanged between the adults. The two 'Thomases' fidget and pull faces at each other.

"But of course, as I have met your guardians before, that cannot be the case here, can it?" Lucy's smile lies on a sandbank waiting for unwary swimmers. "So, to make quite, quite sure, would you both please tell me your middle names? Fletcher, you are the older, you go first."

Silence. The boy opens and closes his mouth like a stranded cod.

"Yes?" Lucy queries gently. "Maybe you didn't hear me, Fletcher. What is your middle name? And Eliza, what is your middle name?"

Both youngsters turn desperate faces to the overseer, whose mouth has fallen open in shock. Lucy picks up a pencil and taps it on the desk. "We are wasting time," she says crisply. "So let me make it clear: either these

ARE the two children of Mr. Sam Thomas, in which case they should know their own baptismal names, both of which Mr. Thomas has told me, or they are not. Which is it?"

"Now then, young woman," the overseer bluffs, "these pore children have suffered so much since they ran away. You can't expect them to remember everything, can you?"

Lucy waves a dismissive hand. "Nice try, but I am afraid it won't wash. They don't even look like Fletcher and Eliza Thomas."

"Here, how do you know that, miss?" the overseer's wife is stung into action as she sees the big reward walking off into the distance. "You nivver met them. We looked after them for years, so we should know what they look like and if we say these are Liza and Flitch, you can take our word for it."

In response, Lucy goes to a cupboard, from which she takes a rolled-up piece of cream paper. She spreads it on the desk. "On the other hand, I might choose to take the word of this artist, who painted both children while they lodged in his house for a while. Here are Eliza and Fletcher Thomas. As you can see, they bear no resemblance whatsoever to the two children you are trying to palm off onto me. The game is up, I'm afraid. And now, we have concluded our business so I must ask you all to leave my office forthwith. Failure to do so will result in my sending out for a constable." Lucy rolls up the painting. "Good day to you," she says firmly, nodding towards the door.

The overseer's wife looks as if she might try to prolong the conversation, but the two children do not wait to be invited to leave a second time. Muttering threats on the lines of "you wait till our Pa finds out about this", they push the overseer aside and make a bolt for the street door. The overseer hauls his wife to her feet and drags her after them.

"It's over," he says. "Better make a move. She means it. We don't want to tangle with the p'lice."

"But where's our reward?" the wife's voice echoes back plaintively as the pair stumble down the stairs.

Lucy waits until she hears the front door slam behind them. She goes to the window and looks down. The two children have completely vanished. The overseer and his wife appear to be having a blazing row in the middle of the pavement. She waits until the street is quite clear of her visitors, then returns to her desk.

In her brief career as a private consulting detective, Lucy Landseer has never defaulted on an inquiry. Her record of success is impeccable, as the testimonials from satisfied clients prove. But now, for the first time, a scintilla of doubt, faint like the smoke from a far-off bonfire, starts to steal over her. She begins to see the impossibility of finding Eliza and Fletcher in all the hustle and bustle of London, with its thousands of cramped alleyways and courts.

Everything she can think of doing to locate the two youngsters has been tried. She has put advertisements in the newspapers, she has hired a couple of sandwich board men to parade up and down Regent Street and Oxford Street, she has even paid for posters to be affixed to walls. She has toyed with going to the police, but as the youngsters have committed no crime, she does not think they would be interested. She is spending Mr. Thomas' money freely but achieving nothing.

The unpleasant couple from the Cambridge Union Workhouse were her best hope. Short of scouring the streets herself, an impossible task, she does not see any way of finding them. Meanwhile, a young lady wishes to hire her on a breach of promise matter. Another fears her family is trying to marry her off against her will.

Both want her to investigate their circumstances urgently.

With a heavy heart, Lucy Landseer admits to herself that she has failed. All that remains is to do what she can to mitigate the situation: she must apologise and send the portrait to Mr. Thomas as the only evidence of the children he once had but now might be lost to him forever. It grieves her on so many levels, but after much reflection, and short of a miracle, she decides that it is the only course left to her.

Her mind made up, Lucy writes a carefully worded letter to Sam Thomas explaining precisely what she has done to locate Fletcher and Eliza. She leaves things open-ended, after all, one never knows. Then she wraps letter and painting in brown paper, ties it with string, applies sealing wax and addresses it to Mr. S. Thomas at his New York place of business, after which she puts on mantle, bonnet and gloves and sets off for the main post office.

****

Detective Constable Tom Williams is up bright and early thanks to the thinness of his mattress and the incessant din from the factories nearby, which meant his sleep was fitful. He is the first down to a breakfast which consists of a variety of local delicacies such as blood pudding and thin squares of charred bread that remind him of rooftiles.

Fortified by this fare, he sets off to stretch his legs and prepare himself for his meeting with Mr. Glossop. Even at this early hour, the air is heavy with sooty smoke. Tom's perambulations take in ill-paved streets lined with back-to-back houses, their windows broken or begrimed. Last night's rain still trickles down from roofs, making pools in the unswept streets. The whole area around the station seems to consist of squalid slums built to house the working classes.

Wherever Tom goes, he is accompanied by the noise of hammers and machines. They never cease, much like the population, who swarm past him on either side in an endless tide of shabbily-dressed, sickly-faced humanity. Nobody makes eye contact, nobody speaks. The entire population seems sunk into some sort of grim private nightmare. At one time, Tom is astonished to encounter a group of men with red eyes and green hair (he finds out later that they are employed in a brass works). His walk takes him past great brick-built factories with high windows and tall chimneys spewing black smoke so that the horizon is partly hidden in lead-coloured clouds.

Eventually the time rolls around for his meeting. He makes his way to the address on the letter and inquires at the front desk for the Chief Constable. Tom is directed to one of the long wooden benches and asked to wait. The Chief Constable is dealing with an urgent matter, he is informed, but will be with him shortly. Nothing much changes, he thinks wryly, remembering how many times he has directed a member of the public to wait on the Anxious Bench in similar circumstances. Now it is his turn.

Tom sits, studying the Wanted posters on the whitewashed walls. Every now and then, the door swings open and a uniformed constable hurries in, frequently accompanied by a worried or truculent citizen. Brief intense conversations take place at the desk. Sometimes the citizen then joins him on the bench, where they sit shoulders hunched, head down, taking a great interest in the grime on the floor; sometimes they are squirreled away to some inner room, presumably to be interrogated.

Tom tries not to fixate on the large clock behind the desk, reminding himself that he is on his own time, and they are doing him a favour. Finally, a door to one side of the desk opens, revealing a short, portly man with a gold watchchain prominently displayed across an ample stomach, and moustaches and side whiskers that went out of fashion many years ago. At the sight of him, the desk constable straightens up and assumes a very busy expression. The man goes up to the desk, exchanges a few words and is nodded in Tom's direction. Tom rises to his feet.

"Now then," the man says, by way of greeting. "You'll be Detective Williams from Scotland Yard in London, I take it?"

Tom confirms the assumption.

"I'm Chief Constable Glossop." The man looks him up and down. Tom can almost see the 'bit young for a detective' thoughts floating in the air above his head. "Inquiring about the Barrowclough factory?"

Tom agrees with the premise.

"If you'd like to follow me then."

Tom does so.

"First time in Birmingham?" Glossop asks, as he shows Tom into a sparsely furnished office. Tom nods. "And how do you find it so far?"

Tom has taken part in too many interrogations to allow himself to be caught in that trap. "It is certainly a busy place," he says diplomatically.

"Busy? I should say it is busy, young man," Glossop says. "Do you know what they call this place? The Workshop of the World! Now, what do you think of that for a title? Could London come up with a title like that? I doubt it."

Tom doubts it too. From what he has seen on his walk, the filth, squalor, piles of coal and ordure, the incessant noise and the huge carts labouring to and fro beat anything his birthplace could offer. And that is saying a lot.

"Not that we're perfect, no, we have our faults, same as any other town," Glossop continues, warming to his theme. "There's poverty ~ yes, we have our share, and there's crime and there's folk who could do better for themselves but choose to live on charity and idleness. But you look at any steam train, any sewing machine, any umbrella, any pen or pen nib and you'll find 'made in Birmingham' inscribed somewhere." The little man swells like a turkey cock. "I'm proud of this town. I was born in it, I worked my way up in it and when I die in it, I expect to be buried over in Edgbaston cemetery."

Tom Williams hopes his expression conveys sincerity. He wonders when he will be given the information he has come so far to obtain.

"Now then, young man ~ you want some information. I have some information." Glossop pulls a folder towards him and opens it. "Here is the address of Mr. George Barrowclough's factory. Not that it is called that anymore, not since Jabez Hale took it on a few years back. J. & O. Hale, it is known as now. I suggest you pay them a visit. They may have documents from the former owner. Which reminds me," he leans across the desk, "what is the exact nature of your inquiry? You didn't mention it in your letter."

"My inquiry concerns the son, Mr. James William Malin Barrowclough."

Glossop's eyes widen. "He that ran away to London, and nivver returned? What, has he turned up after all these years?"

"I'm afraid he has been murdered."

Glossop sits back. "Well, I won't say I'm sorry. The shame of it ~ leaving your family to gad off to a place like that and then nivver a word. His father was half the man he used to be after that young man upped and left. Betrayal, you see. Hits a man hard, that does. Especially when it's your own flesh and blood doing it. Broke him."

"You knew the family?"

"Only through meetings at the Central Hall. They kept themselves to themselves. Very private. Have you caught the man who did it?"

Tom shakes his head. "Not yet. We ~ that is I ~ think the reason for the killing lies in his past, and if we can explore it, we might be able to understand the motives of the murderer."

Glossop pulls a wry face. "Well, lah de dah! Explore the past! Understand the motives! Is that how you London coppers conduct your business? Here we arrest them, try them and either lock them up or hang them. Ah well. London, eh? A different world. So, here's the information you asked for. And now, if you'll excuse me, I have a meeting with the Mayor and the Aldermen about the proposals for the new Council House, so if it's all the same to you, I'll bid you good day and leave you to your 'exploration', Detective Williams."

Tom utters his thanks, picks up the folder, and with a slight inclination of his head (for propriety's sake), makes his way back out into the noisesome, noxious thoroughfare. He walks until he finds a clean and economical coffee house. He enters, orders a cup, and sits down to read through the document folder, underlining parts that seem immediately relevant to his search. His coffee drunk, Tom sets off to find the factory owned by J. & O. Hale. He remembers the game he played with the children on his railway journey. Like brave Sir Handkin, he is also on a quest. In his case, though, the end is the discovery of the truth behind the bizarre persecution and murder of James William Malin Barrowclough.

****

Meanwhile, several hundred miles away, what could be described as a kind of reverse quest is taking place. Having lost access to the reward they'd convinced themselves was there for the taking, the overseer and his wife have returned in ignominy to The Ships Head, minus the two youngsters they set out with. Harsh words have been exchanged with the landlord over the absence of the two juvenile fakes, who are now footloose and fancy free somewhere in the city.

"And I ain't a-tellin' their parents, so don't ask," the landlord snarls at his crestfallen brother-in-law. "You got them into this scrape, so you can get them out of it."

Luckily for all concerned, the two Klems have used their initiative, and reappear towards late afternoon, fed and watered by various kindly hands on their homeward journey, and in possession of a few snitched items.

Blood being thicker than water (or the soup served at The Ships Head), hatchets are soon buried, and once last orders are called, and the public house shuts, the four conspirators get together in the back parlour to plan the next move in the campaign.

"At least we know there ain't nobody else trying to palm off any brats," the landlord's wife says.

"Nor can they," her sister nods. "That detective woman's got a painting of them. We saw it. Spitting image of them it was. If she didn't have it, she'd have believed the Klem children were Liza and Flitch, no doubt whatsoever."

"Suppose they've moved on though?" the landlord muses. "Chances are you won't find them again. London's a big place. They could be anywhere. Maybe they even left the city, you thought about that?"

The overseer has thought about that, but not for long, because it is a thought he doesn't want to think about. "Look, the way I see it, the girl will have gone to ground somewhere nearby, waiting for the boy," he says. "I'm betting, she doesn't know he escaped, so she'll be hanging around keeping watch on this place on the off chance she gets a sight of him. All we have to do is keep an eye out for her. Then when we catch her, we put the word round, and that'll bring the boy running straight into our trap."

The landlord nods. "Sounds like a plan. You say the detective had a painting. Did Lil and Art see it? They did. Good. They can start asking round the neighbourhood, see if anybody's spotted two strange kids turning up out of the blue. No parents in tow." He holds up a hand, "Now then, I just remembered something." He leaves the room, returning a short while later carrying a cap. "The boy left this when he escaped. We'll give it to Art to wear."

The overseer makes a mouth. "Will them kids want to help after what happened this morning?"

"If you pay them, they will, believe me. Sell their own grandmother for the right price. So, what do you say? Your runaways know you, but they don't know Lil and Art. So they won't be looking out for them."

The overseer's wife pulls her husband by the sleeve and whispers in his ear.

"We agree," he says. "Just as long as we find them quickly. We got to get back to work soon."

The landlord raises his glass. "Let's drink to the plan, then. To success and money!"

They raise their glasses. There is a sudden loud crash just outside the window. The overseer's wife almost spills her drink with shock. "What was that?" she exclaims.

"Nothing. Cats, I reckon," the landlord says calmly. "They sometimes try to get into the bins round the back. No cause for alarm. Now drink up and we'll go over the plan again, just to make sure it's shipshape and really watertight."

****

While the plotters are plotting, not a few streets away, Flitch has been given temporary sanctuary at the Chinese Mission House by Pastor Wang in exchange for helping out with daily chores. These involve sweeping out the reading room and replacing the newspapers. Also keeping an eye on the baggage rooms, where the sailors off the ships store their possessions in between voyages.

For these chores he is paid in bowls of tasty food, and in the evening, he and the Wang children are allowed to mix with the guests, listening wide-eyed to their stories of sea-journeys, of the great whales that inhabit the deep oceans of the world, and of the rare delicacies like ginger, amulets, little jade statues, silk and oil for sacred lamps that they bring back with them to sell.

Flitch has noticed that the sailors, many of whom speak English, usually stay for a few days before embarking on their next sea voyage. Those who remain ashore for longer carry with them their own bedding and prefer to sleep with their shipboard companions in the same room. He also gathers that Pastor Wang is held in high esteem by everyone in the crowded thoroughfares around Limehouse and Poplar, where the Chinese community lives and shops and tries to avoid too much contact with the indigenous inhabitants. A constant stream of men and women drop into the Mission House to chat, settle disputes or beg favours.

Every morning, the small gang of youngsters meet with him to plot their surveillance tactics. Flitch longs to join them on the street, but on Li Wei's advice, is confined to the Mission House for the time being. It is hard to know that his sister is out there somewhere, probably desperate to find him, yet he can do nothing but sweep, clean and trust in the good offices of others.

And always, lurking at the back of his mind, is the fear that the longer they take, the better the chances of the overseer, his wife or the police finding her first.

****

A fine sooty rain is falling as Detective Constable Tom Williams alights from the rackety, stale-smelling omnibus that has transported him from the centre of town to the industrial area of Dale End, a short distance away, where the factory of J. & O. Hale is located. He traverses the narrow footway, avoiding the handcarts and wheelbarrows that roll against the kerbstone. He passes a crowd standing around a baker's horse laden with two panniers of bread, and skirts round more heaps of coal and mud.

There is a family of Italian ballad singers on one corner, dressed in rags, their faces gaunt and sunken, bravely singing some jaunty ditty. Their warbling is being mocked by a group of idle boys, who hoot and caper. Tom, recognising starvation when he sees it, clears them away with a peremptory command, then drops some coins into a cup held in the trembling hand of the smallest child.

He walks on, now passing through an area of small workshops, from which emanate the hum of sewing machines and the tap-tap of hammers. From these low buildings emerge a steady stream of men carrying garments or boxes of goods on their way to the railway station. A few aproned workers stand around smoking or eating rough-cut sandwiches. They eye the tall young man curiously, but as Tom, like all members of his profession, gives off an invisible air of policeman, they quickly avert their gaze and look away.

Eventually, he arrives at the iron gates of the factory. Smoke belches out of its chimneys and even with the big entrance doors closed, the sound of machinery seems to fill the street with vibration. Tom pulls on the bell rope and after several minutes an elderly, bleary-eyed man, bent almost double with age, shambles round a corner of the building. He is armed with a fearsome broom and seems not to be fully in possession of his wits. He peers up at Tom Williams, listens to his introduction, then leads him silently to a small side door, standing aside to let him go through.

Tom finds himself in a vast high-ceilinged room with row upon row of huge machines moving back and forth. They are being fed and tended by an army of overalled workers, who pay him no mind whatsoever. Their faces are expressionless; they remind Tom of automata. The noise is deafening and the air redolent with a sharp ferrous smell that recalls the scent of blood. At one end of the factory floor is a vast red furnace, roaring its presence. A group of men are pushing trays of liquid silver into its maw. Nobody speaks, though Tom notices that some form of communication is happening by the amount of strange hand gestures and words silently being mouthed.

After a minute or so, his presence is noticed and a man in a cloth cap and brown overall approaches. Under the overall, he wears a black suit and a black tie. "Yes, mister? What will you?" he shouts.

Tom indicates that he cannot hear him above all the noise. The man beckons him to a small side room and closes the door. He does not offer him a chair. "Now then," he says briskly. "Are you the detective policeman come up from London? We were told you would be visiting."

Tom nods. "I am here seeking personal information about the Barrowclough family, who used to own this factory," he says.

The man shakes his head. "Afraid you've wasted your time, mister. I'm Obadiah Hale; my father bought the works from George Barrowclough some years ago. It was all done fair and square. I've searched the records for you and apart from the legal agreement, there's nothing about the family here. You are welcome to look around if you want, but you'll not find anything. It was all cleared out and burned when we took over. New broom and all that." He shrugs. "I'm sorry, but that's the way of it."

Tom Williams bites down his disappointment. "So you can tell me nothing about the actual Barrowclough family? Nothing at all?"

Hale spreads his hands. "You'd have had to ask my father about that. I never knew them."

"And where would I find him?"

He laughs harshly. "In the cemetery. He died last year."

There is a brief silence while Tom Williams processes what he has learned, which is that he has learned nothing. Then he turns to the door. "Well, I'll be on my way then."

"Might be best thing. Safe journey back to the smoke. Like I said, I'm sorry I couldn't help you, officer," Hale says. He picks up a clipboard and prepares to return to the factory floor. "You can find your own way out, I presume?"

Tom bites back a sarcastic comment. He crosses the noisy factory floor, resisting the temptation to cover his ears, and walks towards the small side entrance, where the old man with the broom is waiting. To Tom's surprise, instead of opening the door, the man plucks him by the sleeve.

"Wait a bit, young master. Not so fast, eh."

Tom stops. The old man mumbles something, wipes a dribble of spittle from his chin, and stares down at his twisted fingers as if he isn't sure who they belong to. He breathes in wheezily a couple of times, coughs, spits something dark brown and disgusting into a corner. "You want to know about the Mr. Barrowclough who owned the fact'ry before this lot took it over, is that right?"

Tom stares down at him. "How do you know that?"

The old man's eyes narrow. "I may be just the sweeper-upper around here, but I still got all my facilities. I can hear. And I heard as how a policeman from London was coming up to arsk about the old master."

"You heard quite right. I asked, but I wasn't told anything," Tom tells him.

The old man scratches his stubbly chin. "Werl, no, happen you wouldn't be. Coz none of them in there," he gestures with a stubby finger, "knows their arse from their elbow, if you gets my meaning. Money is all they know. Money and getting drunk and lasses."

Tom is beginning to see where this is leading. "But you aren't like them, are you?"

"Too right I ain't," the old man chuckles throatily, bringing on another bout of furious coughing and hawking. "I been working here sixty years, boy and man. Started off cleaning under the machine when I was eight. Then I got to working the machines. Then when I got too slow on my feet, the new masters put me to sweeping and caretaking. Anything you wants to know about Mr. Barrowclough as was, or his fambly, you should arsk me. Yus. Coz I know all about them. Oh yus. I knows it all." He nods and pokes Tom in the ribs in a facetious manner.

Tom's eyes widen. So there is something unusual the family's past. He reaches into his inner pocket. The old man waves him away. "Not now. Not here. Now, listen, young man, you come back after five, when this lot have gone home. Pull on the bell three times, so I know it's you. I got a little lean-to shed round the back where I live. It's private. I'll take you there and tell you what you want to know."

Tom's face brightens. "Thank you, Mr. …?"

"Medlar. Like the froot. But you can call me Albert if you like. And you might bring a couple of bottles of beer with you. Helps with the talking, does beer."

Tom's step is light and his heart buoyant as he quits the factory and walks back to his lodgings. He was right: the secret to the strange events surrounding the murder of James William Malin Barrowclough does lie in his past. And in a few hours' time, he, Tom Williams, is finally going to find out exactly what it is.

****

Back in Limehouse, Liza Thomas is also finding out things. In her case, it is that there is more to being a menial drudge than she could possibly have imagined. Life in the Union Workhouse was tough, but at least she was surrounded by other girls her own age. She had friends. And there were always hiding places where she could go when life became too arduous, and other victims who'd be picked on in her stead.

Here, on the other hand, at the *Sailors' Rest: Superior Rooms for Mariners. Prop. C. Dixon*, she finds herself right at the bottom of the food chain. All the other workers are older; they know the ropes and the dodges, and they are only too glad to let the heaviest burdens fall onto her young shoulders. From the moment she rises to the moment she drops utterly exhausted, onto the kitchen floor at night, Liza is harried from pillar to post.

Somehow, without her saying anything, word has got round that she is a fugitive from justice. A runaway from the law. Someone who is only being protected on the basis that she does all the scrubbing, the grate raking, the coal scuttling, the dirty plate scraping and the emptying of the slop pails and night commodes.

And if any of the tasks do not meet with satisfaction, there is a stinging slap round the side of her head from whoever set the task. Liza is busy from dawn to dusk. There is no opportunity afforded her to go out and search for Flitch. Slowly, it dawns on her that she is now virtually a prisoner. There is no escape.

One dull afternoon, Liza finally decides that she has had enough. She is not going to be reunited with her brother at this rate. Perhaps he has given up looking for her? The thought that she might never see him again lies like a stone inside her chest. She simply has to leave, whatever the risk to her personal safety.

And as if Fate has chosen to give her a Get Out of Jail Free card, her decision coincides with the unexpected arrival in the kitchen of Mrs Dixon, looking for somebody to go and fetch the bread order. In the *Sailors' Rest*, the bread order is always collected late afternoon, when it is going stale, and therefore cheaper.

Outside, the weather is turning colder and nastier. None of the staff fancy trekking to the bakers today. Besides, a pot of tea has just been made. Fingers are pointed at Eliza. "She'll go," says the cook, settling down with a copy of the local paper.

Thus, Liza is handed a big wicker shopping basket and given directions. "And don't you go dawdling in the streets, my girl, or it'll be the worse for you when you get back," she is told, a slap accompanying the instructions.

Liza fetches her shawl and her bonnet and leaves the lodging house. Fog is beginning to roll in from the river and the air smells of rot and damp and despair. She quickens her pace, the basket jouncing on her arm. Her intention is to abandon it in the street and make a run for it as soon as she is well clear of the *Sailors' Rest*. Suddenly she stops dead in her tracks, her heart in her mouth. There is a boy standing by a nearby jetty, watching some lighters chugging upriver. She recognises the set of his thin shoulders and the cap he wears. Forgetting her intention, she drops the basket and runs towards him, joyously exclaiming, "Flitch! I found you at last!"

The boy spins round. Liza realises she is looking into the face of a complete stranger. She mutters an apology and begins to back away, but to her horror, the boy comes after her. He reaches out a long skinny arm, and grabs hold of her wrist. "'Ello Eliza," he grins, showing a mouth of crooked yellow teeth. "I fink I found YOU!"

Liza's reaction is instinctive and fast: she bends down and sinks her sharp teeth into the boy's hand. She bites down hard. The boy screams. Liza pulls her arm free and takes to her heels. The boy follows her, yelling curses and commanding passers-by to "stop that girl; she's a thief!"

Liza scurries round corners, slips down back alleyways, sprints across courtyards. Her only purpose is to shake off her pursuer. But the boy has longer legs and he also knows the lie of the land better than she does. Breathless, her heart thudding in her chest, she skids past a row of strange shops adorned with inscriptions and advertisements in Chinese characters. She hears footsteps hurrying up behind her. In desperation, Liza leans against the door of one of the mysterious shops. It opens immediately, pitching her headlong inside.

Liza lies sprawled on her front on the wooden floor of the shop. She is completely winded. She buries her face in her arms, tensing every muscle, waiting for her pursuer to pounce. Nothing happens. Gradually, as her breath returns, she becomes aware of a strange shuffling sound. She sits up. There is a Chinese man dressed in a flowing robe watching her. He has black eyes, a long black pigtail and soft, thick felt shoes.

She scrambles to her feet, her hands automatically forming into fists. The man gives her a half-smile. He nods, beckoning her to follow him. Liza decides she might as well do as he indicates. The boy is probably waiting for her outside the shop. The Chinese man leads her behind the counter, and through a leather curtain into a shadowy back room lit by faint glimmers of light from a couple of small lamps. There are beds and divans, some occupied by prone figures, barely recognisable in the semi darkness. The air is thick with smoke and smells spicy-sweet and oppressive.

The man takes Liza to a small side room, where there is a table, two chairs and numerous shelves containing bowls, small tubes and pipes, tin boxes and packets. He indicates that she is to sit down and wait. Liza sits. The man leaves. Through a crack in the door, she hears a whispered conversation taking place in a language she doesn't understand. Then footsteps recede into the distance.

Time passes. Liza tries to stay alert, but to no avail. Days of unceasing drudgery take their toll and despite her best efforts, tiredness overwhelms her. She tries to focus on the day's events ~ how did the boy who was chasing her know her name? Why was he wearing Flitch's cap? But her eyelids feel heavy, her head begins to loll sideways and soon she slips into an exhausted and uneasy sleep.

She wakes with a start, snatched back to consciousness by a sound. It is pitch dark in the room, but light under the door and the sound of voices drawing nearer shows that someone is coming. She sits upright, wrapping her shawl around her shoulders. The Chinese man enters carrying a lantern, and with him, an older Chinese man, who studies her face intently. Friend or foe, Liza wonders. She does not realise she has spoken the words aloud until the man smiles at her. "Friend," he says. "Yes, Miss Eliza Thomas, definitely a friend. I am Pastor Wang of the Chinese Mission House, and if you trust me, and will come with me now, there is somebody waiting there who is very eager to see you again."

****

Detective Constable Tom Williams returns to his dingy hotel room to await the arrival of five o'clock. He spends the interim writing up his next report for Mr. Greig (whom he is sure will be eager to read how he is getting on), and studying the Police Manual. Outside, great machines hammer away, while every now and then, the sound of a shift clocking off or a shift clocking on brings the voices of workers and the clatter of their boots filtering in through the ill-fitting window of his room. Eventually, when the afternoon fades into early evening, he sets out to meet with the old man, stopping off at a public house on the way to buy the requested libation.

Tom's arrival at the factory gates coincides with the arrival of the early evening shift. He slips through the gates between a couple of grey-faced blank-eyed men who show no interest in him whatsoever and makes his way round to the back where, in the shadow of the high brick wall surrounding the factory, he spies a small wooden windowless shed, that seems to have been nailed together by a child with a random assortment of nails and very little carpentry skills.

He knocks on the plank that serves as a door. After a lot of coughing and muttered curses, the plank slides open to reveal the old man. Tom wrinkles up his nose at the smell of overbreathed air and unwashed body that accompanies him.

"Ah. Good. It's you," the old man mutters. "You better come in. Got the drink?"

Tom lets the bottles chink in his overcoat pocket. A toothless grin overspreads the old man's face. "Now there's a cheery sound, young ...?"

"Tom."

Albert Medlar beckons him over the threshold. The noise from the factory makes the tiny shed vibrate. "Sit you down, Mr. Tom. We ain't fancy round here, so just perch where you can. Mind Puss ~ she don't like strangers. I keep her coz she's a good ratter. We get a lot of rats round here."

A large black and white cat jumps down off a three-legged sofa, gives Tom a disdainful stare, and heads for the door, tail erect. Tom takes her place on the sofa, placing the bottles of beer onto an upturned crate that functions as a table.

Albert Medlar uncorks the first, smacking his lips and takes a long pull at the neck of the bottle. "That's more like it," he says mushily, wiping his mouth on his coat sleeve. He settles back into an antique spoon-back chair with faded gilding and a worn crimson velvet seat. From its incongruous presence, Tom guesses that it must have once belonged to some affluent house. He catches Tom's eye and grins. "Like my chair? I pinched it from Mr. Barrowclough's office after his death. The way I look at it, he worked me to the bone for years, and he paid starvation wages, so I reckoned I was due something for all my hard labour. Anyway, he won't care who's sitting on it where he's gone, will he?"

Tom agrees. The two men sit in companiable silence for a while. Tom watches the level in the first bottle go down, wondering how he is going to get Medlar to tell him what he has come to find out. He does not have to wait long.

"So, Mr. Tom, why are the London coppers int'rested in a man who's dead and buried?" Medlar says, reaching for the second bottle.

"His son has been murdered in unusual circumstances," Tom says. "We are unable to find the man who did it, so we are seeking answers further afield."

There is a long pause. The old man stares off at nothing, the bottle in his hand. Then he says quietly, "His son, you say? Well, I can tell you one thing right off. That man wasn't his real son."

Tom stares at him, thunderstruck. "I'm sorry? Did you just say …"

"You heard me. That man, the one who was murdered in London, he was brought in to take the place of the real one. It was all done secret like. Nobody was supposed to know anything."

Tom opens his notebook and licks the end of his pencil. "Go on, Mr. … Albert," he says.

"It happened when Master James ~ the real son, fell terribly ill with a brain fever," the old man says. He drinks, wipes his mouth on his sleeve. "Would've been about fifteen years old. Away at some fancy boarding school down South at the time. Folk said it was the death of his mama that brought it on. They were always very close. Anyway, his father closed down the family house, got rid of all the servants and left town. Rumour was that he was taking the boy abroad to see a specialist. Put in a manager at the factory ~ nasty piece of work he was.

"Eleven months later, back he comes claiming the boy was completely cured. Sent him off to a different boarding school and that was that. Only my Becky, she'd worked for the family as parlourmaid, happened to see the boy in town getting out of the family carriage that Christmastime and she said she could've sworn it wasn't the same lad. Looked a lot like him, admittedly, but it wasn't him."

Tom waits while the contents of the second bottle follow the first one.

"And did you ever find out whether she was right?" he asks.

The old man gives him a crafty smile. "What do you think?" he says. "Wasn't easy, on account of all the servants being new, but she got to the bottom of it in the end. Seems the master ~ good Christian man that he wasn't, had been carrying on behind his missus' back with some wench. The boy was the result. When the other lad took sick in his mind, he was placed in an asylum and the by-blow was put in his place. Important to have someone to take over the factory, you see. Only in the end, he didn't take over the factory, did he, he just ran off to London. And now he's been murdered, you say? Well, that's justice, ain't it."

Tom is writing so fast there is practically steam coming out of his pencil.

"And the real son ... when did he die?"

The old man shrugs. "Don't know about that. Never heard he was dead. Far as I know, he's still alive, locked away somewhere." He picks up the third bottle. "And that's all what I know, so if it's the same to you, Mr. Tom, I'll say goodnight to you and turn in now. Makes you sleepy, this talking."

The stars are fighting their way through a smoky night sky as Tom walks back to the small hotel, where he has to bang on the door for some time before the night porter appears to grudgingly let him in. Up in his room, Tom throws himself onto the creaky bed and stares at the smoke-blackened ceiling. Earlier, he wrote to Mr. Greig promising that he would be back in London tomorrow first thing, ready to start work once more. But it is abundantly clear now that he won't be.

Next morning, after another unwholesome breakfast, Tom makes his way to Ratcliff Place and mounts the steps up to the grand brick building that houses the central library. He inquires at the desk for a list of lunatic asylums and after a few curious glances from the staff, is given a small maroon leather book.

Tom takes it to one of the tables and begins leafing through its pages, amazed at the number of state and private lunatic asylums that are listed, in alphabetical order, within its covers. He feels bewildered. He cannot possibly inquire at all of these places. And then he turns over a page and sees an entry for: *Magpie House, a private institution for the care, housing and treatment of single male patients of the middle class. All ages. Own attire. No restraints. Fees upon application to Dr. Lucius Sharpe MD.*

Tom's heart jumps. What was it Mr. Greig said about intuition, he thinks? This must surely be the place. The name recalls the dead birds that were sent to Barrowclough by his tormentor. He makes a note of the address, then hands the book back to the library clerk and hurries out of the building. Once outside, Tom hails a cab, climbs aboard, settling his back against the cracked leather upholstery. It is not his usual mode of transport, but he does not have all day to be misdirected by members of the public, half of whom he cannot understand anyway.

The cab takes Tom across town, passing factory after factory interspersed by mean little back-to-back houses. Eventually they stop at the gates of an imposing three-storey stone building on the edge of town. Superficially, nothing hints at its actual purpose, until the visitor looks up and sees barbed wire strung all along the high brick wall that surrounds it.

Tom pays the driver, requests him to wait, then pulls at the bell rope hanging from the wall until a man appears at the doorway, crosses the gravel forecourt and inquires brusquely what his business is. Tom shows him his official warrant card and asks to see the owner. The gate is unlocked, and he is led into the foyer, where there is a high desk and a big ledger ~ two features of every medical institution he has visited in the course of his career.

After a few minutes hanging about in the foyer, looking at all the framed testimonials from grateful patients and their families, a small balding man with a walrus moustache and moist brown eyes appears from within the building. He is accompanied by a younger male orderly. The small man introduces himself to Tom as Dr. Lucius Sharpe. He does not introduce the orderly. Tom Williams shows him his card and asks politely whether they have a patient by the name of Mr. Barrowclough.

The doctor and orderly exchange a worried glance. "May I request the reason why you are asking? Are you a family member?" Dr. Sharpe inquires.

Tom demurs. "I am here in an official capacity. We, that is the detectives at Scotland Yard, are seeking someone in connection with an ongoing investigation. If Mr. Barrowclough is a patient here, I would appreciate being able to question him."

Another worried glance is exchanged. Then the doctor draws Tom aside. "The man is indeed one of our patients. He suffers from delusions and acute melancholia, But I am afraid you cannot question him, officer, for alas he died early this morning of complications resulting from spending many nights out in the open. He had only just returned to us after being absent. He has gone missing before, but never for this length of time. We were about to contact the police ourselves when he reappeared, very much the worse for wear. You say you are from London? That might provide the answer to his destination. And why he came back with his shoes worn to the uppers, his feet cut and bleeding, and his clothes soaking wet. He must have walked all the way from London, sleeping rough."

Tom stares at him. This is not what he was anticipating at all. "I am most sorry to hear this."

"Yes, poor man. He gave us very little trouble. He preferred his own company most of the time. I know little of the original reasons for his incarceration, as it was long before I took over the asylum. He seemed harmless enough. Just a solitary man who had no family or friends to cheer him in his situation. As you are from the London police, would you care to make an examination to see whether he was the man you were looking for?"

Tom nods mutely. He is led along a corridor, with closed doors on either side. His feet sink into pale blue carpet. He follows the doctor up two flights of stairs. Another corridor follows. Finally, the doctor stops at a half open door, through which Tom catches a glimpse of an elderly woman with a basin and a towel.

"Leave that, Sarah, if you wouldn't mind," the doctor says. "I'll send for you when we are finished."

The woman bobs a curtsey, setting the bowl and towel down on the bedside table. Tom steps into the room. It is meagrely furnished; there is a bed, a wardrobe, and a desk, upon which lies a pile of old books, a candle, a quill pen and some pieces of paper.

"If you are ready, officer …"

Tom approaches the bed, steeling himself for what he is about to see. The doctor lifts the sheet, and he glances down, seeing the face of the dead man ~ the full beard and dark hair, just as the French servant described them; just as they appeared in the painting, though the features are terribly sunken, and the skin is the colour of old parchment. He turns away and returns to the desk where he picks up one of the old books. It is an ancient encyclopaedia about British birds.

"This was his book?" he asks.

"Yes, he was very interested in ornithology ~ he actually had a few tame magpies in little wicker cages. We tried to discourage him, but he had so few pleasures in his life. No letters, no visitors, ever. And he kept a scrapbook ~ here it is if you'd like to see it for yourself. We provide a selection of local and national newspapers for our patients to read; it keeps them in touch with the outside world, which we think is important as it helps them to converse when visitors come in."

Tom leafs through the pages. Here are cuttings from the Birmingham Post about pigeon racing and the new railway. Trivial everyday stuff. But on the last page there are two carefully curated pieces: a report about the death of George Barrowclough with a photograph of the dead man, setting out what he was worth, and naming James William Malin Barrowclough 'a London businessman' as the sole inheritor of his wealth and the factory.

Below it is a puff piece from one of the London society papers describing a recent grand Christmas party held at Hill House, the beautiful Hampstead home of the affluent Mr. James William Malin Barrowclough, entrepreneur and land agent. There are photographs of the host and hostess. He closes the scrapbook and hands it back to Dr. Sharpe.

"What will happen to him now?"

"He will be given a Christian funeral. We have a small plot of land in the local churchyard where we bury all the men who've died here, those whose family don't claim them. Unless he's the man you're after, of course ~ obviously we can't carry out a Christian burial for a criminal."

In a future career as one of Scotland Yard's finest detectives, Tom Williams will frequently find himself in situations where the outcome hangs solely upon his decision. Lives and fates will be placed, for good or ill, in his hands. Now, he stares out of the window, his mind sifting possibilities and choices. Then he turns. "No," he says firmly, "I am afraid this isn't the man we are looking for. I am sorry to have wasted your time. Thank you for showing him to me."

****

It is a few days after Flitch and Liza's joyful reunion and here they are sitting in the Chinese Mission House kitchen, warm and safe and together once more. Two bowls of hot soup steam in front of them. On the other side of the table sit Li Wei, Rose and Berthold, listening intently once again to the recounting of dangers averted and rescues enacted.

"It is like the legend of the Bird with Nine Hands," Berthold says.

His brother and sister roll their eyes. "No, it isn't," Rose says. "But never mind."

"So, what happens now?" Li Wei asks. "Our spies tell us that the two Klem children are still on the lookout for you. It is not safe for you to go outside until the hunt has been called off, I think."

Flitch sighs. "We can't stay here forever," he says reflectively. "We might as well be back in the Union ~ no offence to your pa. We have to get away, somehow."

Liza sips her hot soup. "At least we got each other, Flitch," she says. Pauses. "Though I'm sorry I had to sell our things."

Her brother puts an arm round her shoulders. "Things don't matter Liza. We didn't have anything before we escaped. It's people what matters. Good friends who've helped us. We'll find a way to leave here, somehow."

They sit quietly for a while, each engrossed in their own thoughts. Then Pastor Wang comes in and with him is a young man in sailor's clothes, his hair neatly plaited round his head. "This is Ju-long," Pastor Wang says. "He lodges locally with his mother and has been on shore leave. I have been explaining your situation to him. He has an idea."

The young man nods, smiling round at the group. He points towards the window. He points towards Flitch and Liza. He mimes running with his fingers. He mimes climbing a ladder. He mimes sleeping.

"Ju-long is a member of the crew on a ship bound for New York," Pastor Wang translates. "It sails tonight on the evening tide. He suggests dressing you both up in Chinese garments and slipping you out of the back door along with him. Three Chinese people making their way to the harbour will barely merit a second glance. Once you are smuggled on board ship, you will be safe. Nobody will be able to catch you. What do you think of the plan?"

Liza turns to her brother, her eyes shining. "New York, Flitch! Did you hear that! New York is in America! That's where Pa has gone. Oh, say we can go!"

Her brother smiles down at her eager face. "Got to be a better life for us there than here, Liza, that's for sure. We can't keep on running from the police or the workhouse for ever. Sooner or later, someone will catch us, and then it'll be back to the Union, or put in prison." He looks at Pastor Wang and his gaze is steady and determined. "Tell him we'll do it. And say thank you."

Pastor Wang and the young sailor exchange a brief conversation. "It is settled then. If you would like to pack what you need, I shall find some suitable disguises from the mission box and some other bits and pieces to start you out in your new life. We both think the sooner you are on board, the better. Then whenever anybody comes here and orders me to hand you over, I can say with absolute truthfulness that you left the Mission House and I do not know where you are ~ for the sea is very wide indeed, and you could be anywhere upon it."

"But New York is such a long way away," Rose murmurs plaintively. "How will you both survive? How will you eat?"

Flitch takes out his pack of cards, shuffles them and shows her the painted Queen of Hearts. "The lady will provide," he tells her with a mischievous grin. "For the rest, we'll have to wait and see. We've been lucky so far. Come on, Liza, let's collect what we have, and be on our way."

A short while later, just as afternoon is fading silverly into dusk, three figures walk out of the rear of the Chinese Mission House and head for the docks. Each wears a small velvet skull cap, a high buttoned navy jacket and thick felt boots. Each carries a cloth-wrapped bundle over one shoulder. Without making eye contact with anybody they pass, they march in line and at speed towards the basin, where the ship waits, broadside to the wharf. Her name, the Enterprise is painted on her side.

Two spar and plank gangways connect the vessel to the wharf, where groups of fellow voyagers laden with possessions are moving to and fro. They carry cabbages, loaves of bread, wheels of cheese, boxes, beds, bundles, babies, tin cans for water, for this is an emigrant ship and those who are sailing on her are heading for a new life. Small children caper excitedly, are lost, are found again, are slapped, are told to stay with their family but are far too excited to obey.

Ju-long clears a pathway through and they climb aboard. Then he leads them across the main deck and down a ladder to the between-decks of the ship. Here, sailors are stacking bales, chests and barrels ready for the long trip. He indicates a space at the foot of the gangway, where some rope has been coiled, making a secluded nest. Flitch carefully deposits their cloth bundles behind the rope, where they cannot be seen. Then brother and sister make their way back to the top deck to watch the passengers coming on board and to listen to the waves lapping against the pier.

By six o'clock, all of the passengers are safely aboard. Kettles are being heated over small stoves and loaves sliced and buttered. Liza has made friends with a young couple with a fretful baby, whom she is rocking gently while singing to it. Flitch is exploring the ship. Eventually, the vessel slips out of the river and heads for the open sea. Fitch and Liza make up their beds in the coils of rope and fall asleep to the sound of rolling and rushing waves as the great ship ploughs its way across the ocean, under a night of bright silver stars and a dark, cold sky, bearing them onwards to the Bay of New York and the beginning of their next great adventure.

****

Meanwhile, the night mail train carrying Detective Constable Tom Williams back to London pulls into Euston station in the early hours of the morning. Barely has it come to a steaming, huffing halt against the buffers, when it is besieged by porters rushing to unload mail sacks onto trolleys and bear them swiftly out of the station to the waiting cabs, to be unpacked and sorted at the General Post Office, ready for the first deliveries to the city.

Too wired to sleep, Tom has spent the entire journey completing his report for Greig, in the hope that he won't get a reprimand for going well beyond the agreed time of absence. He is also uneasy about how his superior officer will view the contents of the letters he sent against the final choice he made. There is a widow, and her two sons to be considered after all. Now they will never learn how (or why) Barrowclough was murdered.

He arrives at Scotland Yard in good time and hurries straight to Greig's office to place the report on his desk before he comes into work. To his surprise, he sees that his previous letters describing the progress of his investigation are lying on the desk, unopened. Tom goes to find an explanation, which he eventually receives from one of the detective sergeants, newly arrived in the front office.

"Mr. Greig's not been in for several days," he tells Tom. "His wife's given birth to a boy. Herbert John Lachlan, they've called him. Don't think he'll be interested in what you've got to show him. Other more important things on his mind."

"Maybe Mr. Stride then ...?" Tom suggests.

The officer grins, "Doubt he'll be interested either, mate. He's just informed the whole police office that he's going to hang up his boots at Easter. Retiring at last. Wants to spend more time in his garden and writing his memoirs, which I for one, won't be reading. He's far too busy right now getting all the paperwork in place to bother about whatever you've been up to. So if you'll take my advice, go and file that report in the basement, and then come up to the officers' room. We're having a whip-round for the new baby and deciding which public house we're going to go to after work to whet the little lad's head. Good times, eh: a new nipper for Mr. Greig and old grizzle-guts is off at last. Hurry up, then. We'll wait for you to join us."

Bewildered at the unexpected turn of events, Tom takes his report down to the basement and places it at the back of the box file labelled: **Barrowclough Murder, January 1868**. Then he goes back upstairs to join his fellow officers, slipping first into Greig's office, where he picks up the unopened letters and puts them in his pocket. They are not important anymore.

Four months later:
New York: autumn breathing over summer's shoulder, and the trees in the park are turning russet and gold in anticipation. Sidewalks are bustling with New Yorkers going about their daily routines. Shoe-shine boys holler their prices. Fruit carts ply their wares and here, on the corner of a busy Lower East Side Street, where there are more tenements than trees and the air smells of roast meat, horse muck, chimney smoke and the salty tang of the East River, a boy in a battered top hat sits behind a small collapsible table. On the table are a couple of packs of playing cards. The boy selects a pack and performs an elaborate shuffle. As the cards fly through the air, he cries, "Roll up, roll up! Find the queen, ladies and gents. Can you see her? Do you know where she is?"

His English accent and cocky air of bravado soon draws a crowd and before long, money is being put down and cards are being shuffled and placed. A lad carrying rolls of bright dress material hurries by. A Jew in a long gaberdine coat and fur trimmed hat hurries by. Stout matrons carrying baskets hurry by. A nursemaid with a perambulator hurries by. A man in a tweed cap hurries by. And suddenly stops.

The man turns, his glance caught by the girl standing behind the card player. A girl with scattery curls and golden brown, long-lashed tiger-eyes. His gaze goes from the girl to the boy, his eyes widening in shock and disbelief. Time distils to a single heartbeat. The air holds its breath. Then Sam Thomas pushes his way through the crowd.

Finis

Thank you for reading this book. If you have enjoyed it, why not leave a review on Amazon, a comment on social media, or recommend it to other readers? All reviews, however long or short, help me to continue doing what I do.